Anonymous

Celebration of the Hundredth Anniversary of the Birth of Robert Burns

Anatiposi

Anonymous

Celebration of the Hundredth Anniversary of the Birth of Robert Burns

Reprint of the original.

1st Edition 2023 | ISBN: 978-3-38230-825-4

Anatiposi Verlag is an imprint of Outlook Verlagsgesellschaft mbH.

Verlag (Publisher): Outlook Verlag GmbH, Zeilweg 44, 60439 Frankfurt, Deutschland
Vertretungsberechtigt (Authorized to represent): E. Roepke, Zeilweg 44, 60439 Frankfurt, Deutschland
Druck (Print): Books on Demand GmbH, In de Tarpen 42, 22848 Norderstedt, Deutschland

CELEBRATION

OF THE

HUNDREDTH ANNIVERSARY

OF THE

Birth of Robert Burns,

BY THE

BOSTON BURNS CLUB.

JANUARY 25th, 1859.

BOSTON:
PRINTED BY H. W. DUTTON AND SON,
TRANSCRIPT BUILDING.
1859.

BOSTON BURNS CLUB.

ORIGIN OF THE CLUB.

It is an unique feature of our republicanism that, however humble may be the origin of effort, its promoters for local or general good invariably find encouragement in their operations from men whose approbation is a safe endorsement of true value. It has been so with the Burns Club of Boston, which was constituted nine years ago. It originated among a few persons whose retired position in society afforded them no pretence, beyond their own gratification, in their own simple way, of a feeling which taught them that the commemorating the genius—the intellectual example—the freedom of mind and action—the patriotic independence—the nobility of soul and sentiment, and their undying expression by one of their brotherhood in humility, was a virtue. The advent of the Club was no sooner known than the mighty of mind, the good, generous, and influential, voluntarily rallied around its purpose, and gave it strength and reputation far beyond what its originators had ever contemplated—and they were not destitute of any proper enthusiasm. Every year gave it renewed influence in the number and social standing of its members; and now, when it has overcome its Ninth, and most marked, Anniversary Festival, the Club can boast of between two and three hundred names on its roll of men whom any association might own with pride. There has never been any national, sectional, or other bar to membership. To be a true admirer of Robert Burns has ever been the foremost qualification; and the uninterrupted harmony of the Association, from its inception to the present hour, has proved that this single qualification brings in its train all other essentials of good membership.

Prior to 1850, when the Club was first organized, parties had frequently met to celebrate the Birthday of Burns; but these celebrations were the results of impulses begotten on occasion, and gratified, to be revivified or not as errant chance might suggest. We know of no associated Burns Club or society before our own had its origin—although attempts were several times made to that end without permanence of result. Two or three individuals, who are now our oldest members, and who had vainly endeavored to effect some systematic plan of association, met and talked the matter over, and their deliberations culminated in the determination to establish, if possible, a Literary and Social Club, under the title which our society bears. In this shape they deemed that they could draw together men, the cultivation of whose literary tastes formed their principal enjoyment—men who would delight in discussing the classical, local, and general value of the poetical literature of Scotland and America, and in quietly and unassumingly constituting their little band the nucleus around which their friends, who might be less ardent in their devotion to such matters, might rally once a year to celebrate the birth of BURNS. They put their resolution into practice; and no sooner, as has been stated, was this made known, than men came to their support whose patronage was true encouragement, and all at once the little fireside association sprung into enviable repute, which has increased with its years. Three men, nine years ago, were its humble and unpretending foster-fathers: to-day the BURNS CLUB of Boston has for its members nearly two hundred and fifty men—among them some of the greatest minds which adorn the literature of the day, the forum, the bar, the learned professions generally; and "last, not least," men who, in the humbler walks of life, are eminent among the practically good and virtuous!

Thus premising, we take up the written record of the proceedings of the Club, of which the following is an abstract, showing in brief its transactions up to the period of its special pride, when, on the 25th of January last, its Celebrative Festival was crowned with a success which has rarely if ever had a parallel in the history of such assemblages.

BOSTON, FEBRUARY, 1859.

RECORD OF THE CLUB.

The primary meeting, held to constitute the Club, took place in the Stackpole House, on the evening of the 11th of January, 1850. It was privately convened to take preliminary steps "for the establishment of a literary and social club, to be called by such name as might hereafter be agreed upon." James Egan, counsellor-at-law, was called to the chair; John C. Moore, James Kelt, Jr., Robert Torrance, William Schouler, William Mitchell, and James Egan were appointed a committee to draft a Constitution and By-Laws for the government of the projected association; and Alexander McGregor, John Leishman, Sen., and William A. Weeks were selected to nominate a President, Vice-President, Secretary and Treasurer—both committees to report at a meeting of the parties named, to be held the following Friday evening.

The promoters of the Society met on the evening of January 18th, 1850, in the Stackpole House, when James Egan again presided, and when it was resolved that they should organize themselves as "THE BURNS LITERARY AND SOCIAL CLUB OF BOSTON."

Alexander McGregor, from the nominating committee, reported a list of officers for the Club, as follows, and the parties recommended were unanimously elected :—

President, . . . WILLIAM SCHOULER.
Vice-President, JAMES EGAN.
Treasurer, . . . JOHN LEISHMAN, SEN.
Secretary, . . . JOHN CHARLES MOORE.

Six names were proposed for membership; and the next meeting fixed for the first Wednesday of the following month of February.

The committee appointed to draw up a Constitution, and rules for the government of the Club, made their report, through John C. Moore, and the Preamble and By-Laws annexed were adopted :—

CONSTITUTION.

As admirers of literary genius, under whatever circumstances or auspices it presents itself—and the more especially when its labors have contributed to the moral and social improvement and enlightenment of mankind—We, who subscribe, rank ourselves under the banner of ROBERT BURNS, not with a pride of exclusiveness, but with feelings based on the peculiar affinity between the conduct and sentiments of the Poet of Scotland and those objects, practically and otherwise valuable, which our fraternity desire to aid in carrying out.

When we contemplate the truly upright bearing of BURNS, as, surrounded with varied and heavy trials and difficulties, his master mind, with high moral dignity, rose powerfully above the struggle, our wish is to emulate him, and to incite others also to copy this feature in his character.

We admire, also, the virtuous pride of BURNS. Poverty, persecution, and "the world's cold neglect" could not wrest from him his consistency, or bribe him to sacrifice his deliberate mind to assist or mend his fortune. Should circumstances demand it of us, we would aim to profit by his marked example, and in all cases use it as a shield against temptation to do wrong.

We admire the honest independence of BURNS. Liberty—American liberty!—fought side by side with his sentiments of freedom and manly self-respect, and found in them a powerful ally. Enjoying as we do the full advantages of that liberty of speech and action he was fated to see but partly established, our admiration of their benefits will always be enhanced by associating ourselves with the name of one of their boldest and ablest promoters.

We honor the liberality of sentiment which characterized BURNS. In the face of danger to life and interest he taught and sung that no allegiance was justifiable or due to what was not in itself just, virtuous, and good. His acts gave credit to his speech. In similar respect, in word and in deed, we would desire to emulate him.

We are admirers of the firm and constant friendships of BURNS; for his chequered life shows no sacrifice of any one made between "his cradle and his grave." In our fraternal intercourse we would wish to study and copy this beautiful feature in the character of "the world's poet."

In his domestic qualities we find much worthy of imitation and something to forget: while we would cultivate his virtues in this relation, we hope we shall ever be anxious to shun all his indiscretions.

In a social capacity we would desire to imitate his example in its openness and generosity, the while we hope to avoid its extremes, and discountenance all practices which tend to impede the healthy nurture, or depress the tone, of the mind—practices which but too often serve only to mark the height whence great intelligences may fall. We would hold the errors of BURNS up to our view as lessons the moral promptings of which we would be unwilling to hide from our consciences, or from the perceptions of our brethren, should circumstances justify friendly advice. We look upon the social memory of ROBERT BURNS as a beacon on the path of life, which, while it points out the safer course, also indicates the proximity of danger.

In the formation of our association, we have the direct example of BURNS himself attesting the utility of such societies. He was one of the earliest promoters of such institutions, and his approval of their benefits is on record in his works.

In conclusion, We, who have hereunto subscribed, declare the opinion, that, as it has never been the special privilege of any civilized country in the world to teach, it is not the province of any one merely to hear; and therefore our Society is established on behalf of the ADMIRERS OF BURNS, from whatever country or clime they may date their origin. The whole world has paid honors to the mighty genius whose name our association bears, and we would not, if we could, confine within more circumscribed limits this universal admiration; neither dare we justify ourselves in the attempt to confine the benefits of the mind and example of BURNS within any sectional compass in so far as our organization is concerned. As individuals, and as a fraternity, we hope to go forward and increase in usefulness, so that our association may be valuable because of its purposes, useful in its accomplishments, and respected in its operations and in its memory.

Our objects, we presume, can be best accomplished through the mutual wish to be governed by good motives rather than merely mechanically considered rules of proceeding; but for the purpose of general direction, we agree to be guided by the annexed By-Laws:—

RULES OF GENERAL GOVERNMENT.

Article I. The name of our association shall be "The Boston Burns Club," and the design of its members literary improvement and the cultivation of fraternal sentiment.

Article II. The officers of the Club shall be a President, a Vice-President, a Secretary, Treasurer, and Librarian.

Article III. The annual election of officers shall take place on the first Wednesday in the month of February in each year.

Article IV. The annual social meeting of the Club shall be held on the twenty-fifth day of the month of January in each year; and the ordinary meetings on the first Wednesdays of each alternate month.

Article V. The quarterly meetings, for special business, shall be held on the first Wednesdays of January, April, July, and October, severally, and shall be occasions for the contribution, by members, of papers on literary subjects, or of oral communications concerning the same.

Article VI. The names of candidates for membership shall be proposed at any monthly meeting, and entered in a book provided for that purpose; and, being seconded, shall be balloted for at the ensuing quarterly meeting.

Article VII. No ballot shall be valid unless ten members actually vote, and three black balls shall exclude.

Article VIII. Every person admitted to membership shall sign the Constitution, and pay an entrance fee of two dollars.

ARTICLE IX. These regulations may be altered or amended at any regular monthly meeting by a vote of two thirds of the members present and in quorum: provided that notice has been given of such alteration or amendment at the previous monthly meeting.

NAMES OF MEMBERS.

Name.	Birthplace.	Country.
1. William Schouler,	Kilbarchan,	Scotland.
2. James Egan,	Galway,	Ireland.
3. John Chas. Moore,	Kilmarnock,	Scotland.
4. John Patterson,	Kettle,	Scotland.
5. John Leishman,	Denny,	Scotland.
6. John Wilson,	Glasgow,	Scotland.
7.*James A. Abbott,	Conway, N. H.,	United States.
8.*William A. Weeks,	Portsmouth, N. H.,	United States.
9. Robert Torrance,	Edinburgh,	Scotland.
10. William Bogle,	Glasgow,	Scotland.
11. Alexander McGregor,	Derry, N. H.,	United States.
12. William Mitchell,	Paisley,	Scotland.
13. David Miller,	Perth,	Scotland.
14.*Edward P. Meriam,	Boston, Mass.,	United States.
15. Samuel S. Gilbert,	Hanover, N. H.,	United States.
16.*James Kelt, Jr.,	Boston, Mass.,	United States.
17. Andrew Weddell,	Edinburgh,	Scotland.
18.*John H. Jewett,	Boston, Mass.,	United States.
19. John N. Bradley,	Dracut, Mass.,	United States.
20. William P. Fetridge,	Liverpool,	England.
21. Francis N. Mitchell,	Edinburgh,	Scotland.
22. Timothy O'Keefe,	Fermoy,	Ireland.
23. Justin Jones,	Brunswick, Me.,	United States.
24.*William Chadwick,	London,	England.
25. Newell A. Thompson,	Uxbridge, Mass.,	United States.
26. James Anderson,	Fordel,	Scotland.
27. Peter Low,	London,	England.
28. James Sutherland,	Edinburgh,	Scotland.
29.*John Leishman, Jr.,	Glasgow,	Scotland.
30. Samuel Ritchie,	Belfast,	Ireland.
31. Otis Rich,	Boston, Mass.,	United States.
32.*Allen C. Spooner,	Plymouth, Mass.,	United States.
33. Henry Whitney, Jr.,	Wiscasset, Me.,	United States.
34. Robert Hutcheson,	Greenock,	Scotland.
35. John H. Leighton,	Edinburgh,	Scotland.
36. John R. Stitt,	Belfast,	Ireland.
37. William Leighton,	Belfast,	Ireland.
38. John Kirkpatrick,	Galloway,	Scotland.

Name.	Birthplace.	Country.
39. Peter Donald,	Forfar,	Scotland.
40. Lyman T. Vose,	Boston, Mass.,	United States.
41. Joseph Aitchison,	Kirkudbright,	Scotland.
42. James H. Briggs,	Nantucket, Mass.,	United States.
43. James Williamson,	Edinburgh,	Scotland.
44. John C. King,	Kilwinning,	Scotland.
45. Charles Mitchell,	Aberdeen,	Scotland.
46. George W. Cooley,	Deerfield, Mass.,	United States.
47. John S. Holmes,	New Bedford, Mass.,	United States.
48. John S. Tyler,	Boston, Mass.,	United States.
49. George W. Minns,	Boston, Mass.,	United States.
50. Josiah Swain,	Nantucket, Mass.,	United States.
51. Alexis Poole,	Charlestown, Mass.,	United States.
52. William Stowe,	Springfield, Mass.,	United States.
53. C. F. Lougee,	Walden, Vt.,	United States.
54. John G. Roberts,	Somersworth, N. H.,	United States.
55. S. P. Gilbert,	Hebron, Conn.,	United States.
56. Samuel Hatch,	Boston, Mass.,	United States.
57.*John L. Dimmock,	Barnstable, Mass.,	United States.
58.*Thomas Morgan,	Bristol,	England.
59. R. B. Brown,	Pollockshaws,	Scotland.
60. N. S. Lougee,	Compton,	Canada East.
61. William Ellison,	Philadelphia, Pa.,	United States.
62. Joseph B. Frost, Jr.,	Marblehead, Mass.,	United States.
63. Chas. S. Snow,	Boston, Mass.,	United States.
64. Robert I. Burbank,	Shelburne, N. H.,	United States.
65. Gideon F. Thayer,	Watertown, Mass.,	United States.
66. E. G. Tucker,	Winchendon, Mass.,	United States.
67. John Stiles,	Pictou,	Nova Scotia.
68. John Byers,	Brechin,	Scotland.
69. E. W. Pike,	Hampton Falls, N. H.,	United States.
70. Chas. Lowell Blanchard,	Boston, Mass.,	United States.
71. James Lee, Jr.,	New York,	United States.
72. Edward G. Parker,	Boston, Mass.,	United States.
73. William W. Clapp, Jr.,	Boston, Mass.,	United States.
74. William D. Park,	Bath,	England.
75. Chas. O. Rogers,	Worcester, Mass.,	United States.
76. Samuel O. Aborn,	Boston, Mass.,	United States.
77. George Canning Hill,	Norwich, Conn.,	United States.
78. Sidney Webster,	Gilmanton, N. H.,	United States.
79. George H. Kingsbury,	Kennebunk, Me.,	United States.
80. Francis H. Underwood,	Enfield, Mass.,	United States.
81. Isaac Livermore,	Waltham, Mass.,	United States.
82. Charles P. Bosson,	Salem, Mass.,	United States.
83. Saml. R. Glen,	Philadelphia, Pa.,	United States.
84. Henry G. Parker,	Plymouth, Mass.,	United States.
85. Seth E. Brown,	Exeter, Me.,	United States.
86. Edward L. Davenport,	Boston, Mass.,	United States.
87. Emery N. Moore,	Ellsworth, Me.,	United States.
88. Z. K Pangborn,	Peacham, Vt.,	United States.
89. J. Q. A. Bean,	Moultonborough, N. H.,	United States.

Name.	Birthplace.	Country.
90. Francis D. Stedman,	Lancaster, Mass.,	United States.
91. James Slade,	Boston, Mass.,	United States.
92. George H. Child,	Boston, Mass.,	United States.
93. Isaac F. Shepard,	Natick, Mass.,	United States.
94. Thomas P. Rich,	Lynn, Mass.,	United States.
95. Silas Pierce,	Scituate, Mass.,	United States.
96. Jesse Holbrook,	Wellfleet, Mass.,	United States.
97. Samuel D. Crane,	Boston, Mass.,	United States.
98. James W. Ricker,	Portsmouth, N. H.,	United States.
99. George Dennie,	Boston, Mass.,	United States.
100. George A. Curtis,	Boston, Mass.,	United States.
101. John Schouler,	Kilbarchan,	Scotland.
102. Samuel Hooper,	Marblehead, Mass.,	United States.
103. Eugene Tisdale,	Guildhall, Vt.,	United States.
104. William Lumb,	Huddersfield,	England.
105. Joseph McKean Churchill,	Milton, Mass.,	United States.
106. Henry O. Hildreth,	Dedham, Mass.,	United States.
107. Chas. B. Hall,	Oxford, N. H.,	United States.
108. Moses W. Weld,	Boston, Mass.,	United States.
109. George H. Chapman,	Boston, Mass.,	United States.
110. Benjamin James,	Boston, Mass.,	United States.
111. John Tisdale Bradley,	Boston, Mass.,	United States.
112. Albert J. Wright,	South Hadley, Mass.,	United States.
113. Geo. N. Nichols,	Cumberland, R. I.,	United States.
114. Warren Tilton,	Newburyport, Mass.,	United States.
115. Ralph W. Newton,	Greenfield, Mass.,	United States.
116. John K. Hall,	Boston, Mass.,	United States.
117. William Pearce,	Bath,	England.
118. James M. Shute,	Boston, Mass.,	United States.
119. C. H. Stedman,	Lancaster, Mass.,	United States.
120. G. W. Talbot,	Boston, Mass.,	United States.
121. Osmyn Brewster,	Worthington, Mass.,	United States.
122. Chas. G. Johnson,	Palatine Bridge, N. Y.,	United States.
123. J. Frederick Marsh,	Boston, Mass.,	United States.
124. Alexander H. Rice,	Newton Lower Falls, Ms.,	United States.
125. Geo. O. Brastow,	Wrentham, Mass.,	United States.
126. Geo. W. Messenger,	Boston, Mass.,	United States.
127. Edward Kreisler,	Malaga,	Spain.
128. Francis Adams,	Quincy, Mass.,	United States.
129. Uriel Crocker,	Marblehead, Mass.,	United States.
130. Benjamin F. Palmer,	Hingham, Mass.,	United States.
131. Richard S. Spofford,	Newburyport, Mass.,	United States.
132. D. N. Richards,	Boston, Mass.,	United States.
133. John P. Healy,	Boston, Mass.,	United States.
134. Ezra Lincoln,	Boston, Mass.,	United States.
135. Albert Webster,	Ipswich, Mass.,	United States.
136. Gordon Forrest,	Aberdeen,	Scotland.
137. Roger N. Allen,	Greenfield, Mass.,	United States.
138. Dexter N. Richards,	Boston, Mass.,	United States.
139. John C. Wyman,	Northboro', Mass.,	United States.
140. John Foster,	Warren, N. H.,	United States.

	Name.	Birthplace.	Country.
141.	Moses G. Cobb,	Dorchester, Mass.,	United States.
142.	Harvey Jewell,	Winchester, N. H.,	United States.
143.	William E. Parmenter,	Boston, Mass.,	United States.
144.	E. D. Brigham,	Boston, Mass.,	United States.
145.	James A. Dix,	Boston, Mass.,	United States.
146.	Joseph M. Wightman,	Boston, Mass.,	United States.
147.	Charles Levi Woodbury,	Portsmouth, N. H.,	United States.
148.	John S. Eldridge,	Yarmouth, Mass.,	United States.
149.	Benjamin F. Russell,	Boston, Mass.,	United States.
150.	A. O. Brewster,	Hanover, N. H.,	United States.
151.	Charles Emerson,	Bridgeton, Me.,	United States.
152.	Stephen S. Seavy,	Deerfield, N. H.,	United States.
153.	Henry L. Hallett,	Boston, Mass.,	United States.
154.	John Tyler,	Boston, Mass.,	United States.
155.	Charles R. Train,	Framingham, Mass.,	United States.
156.	Joseph H. Sawyer,	Bolton, Mass.,	United States.
157.	Sanford Howard,	Easton, Mass.,	United States.
158.	Henry A. Snow,	Boston, Mass.,	United States.
159.	Charles H. Dilloway,	Boston, Mass.,	United States.
160.	John A. Baxter,	Yarmouth, Mass.,	United States.
161.	Joseph Smith,	Dorchester, Mass.,	United States.
162.	William T. Glidden,	Newcastle, Me.,	United States.
163.	William J. Eames,	Malden, Mass.,	United States.
164.	Augustus C. Carey,	Ipswich, Mass.,	United States.
165.	Jonas H. French,	Boston, Mass.,	United States.
166.	Charles H. Blanchard,	Boston, Mass.,	United States.
167.	Joseph H. Bradley,	Boston, Mass.,	United States.
168.	Frank B. Fay,	Southboro', Mass.,	United States.
169.	Thomas W. Camm,	Glasgow,	Scotland.
170.	Richard S. Spofford,	Newburyport, Mass.,	United States.
171.	A. B. Merrill,	Boston, Mass.,	United States.
172.	Charles G. Godfrey,	Boston, Mass.,	United States.
173.	Moses Kimball,	Gloucester, Mass.,	United States.
174.	John L. Swift,	Falmouth, Mass,,	United States.
175.	Edwin Adams,	Boston, Mass.,	United States.
176.	William E. Webster,	Plymouth, N. H.,	United States.
177.	George Forrest,	Aberdeen,	Scotland.

[NOTE.—The asterisk (*) preceding names in the above list denotes that the parties have deceased.

The members number 238, but several of them have not signed the Constitution of the Club.]

RECORD OF TRANSACTIONS.

The first meeting of the Club, after its organization, was held on the 6th of February, when the literary merits of

Hogg, the Ettrick Shepherd, were discussed, and several original anecdotes of the author of "Kilmeny" related. The record subsequently shows that similar conversations were had regarding contemporaries of Burns, whose foibles or virtues he had recorded in his works; the customs and manners of the Scottish peasantry at the time the poet lived, &c., &c.

On the 8th November, 1851, the Secretary read the first of a series of papers, entitled "Personal Reminiscences of the Contemporaries of Burns," and continued them during four consecutive months.

At the meeting held on 4th December of same year it was resolved that the Club celebrate the succeeding Anniversary of the Birthday of Robert Burns, and Alexander McGregor, James Kelt, Jr., and William A. Weeks, were appointed a Committee on preliminaries.

On the same evening John Wilson read an Essay on "The Influences of Knowledge and a Literary Taste on the Condition of the Working Classes."

[1851.] At the meeting on the 1st of January, 1851, James Egan read a paper on "The Life and Times of Goethe," and the arrangements for the first annual festival were perfected.

The first Anniversary Celebration by the Club of the Birthday of Burns took place on the evening of the 25th of January, 1851, in the Stackpole House, and proved itself an occasion of much gratification to all present. President William Schouler occupied the Chair. Sixty-three persons sat down to Supper, including the Mayor of the City, and the President of the Senate and Speaker of the House of Representatives.

The second annual meeting for the choice of officers took place on Wednesday evening, February 5th, 1851, when it was reported by the Secretary that the Club was composed of twenty-four active members. The Treasurer reported that the receipts of the Club had been $48, and the expenses during the past year $12, leaving a balance of $36 in favor of the Club. The officers elected for 1851-2 were—

President, . . . William Schouler.
Vice President, James Egan.
Treasurer, . . . John Leishman.
Secretary, . . . John Chas. Moore.

At this meeting a proposition was made that the Club endeavor to procure copies of all the principal editions of the Poems of Robert Burns, published in Europe and America, and a special committee, consisting of John C. Moore, John Wilson and William A. Weeks, appointed to make enquiry and report on the subject.

At the meeting held on March 5th, 1851, the President and Secretary were authorized to communicate with Provost Frazer of Dumfries, Scotland, relative to the public subscription set on foot for the repair of Burns's mausoleum at Dumfries.

At the monthly meeting, held on the 2nd of April following, a very animated discussion arose concerning certain remarks contained in one of the papers read by the Secretary on Burns and his Contemporaries. The prevailing feature of debate was the defence of the reputation of the Poet against the prejudices of his contemporaries, which had led them into uncharitableness and detraction. The paper which caused the discussion, as also those of the series, by request of the Club, were placed at its disposition, with the proviso that they should not be published.

At the succeeding meeting, held on the 6th of May, a committee was appointed to revise the By-Laws of the Club. Allen C. Spooner recited two original poems prepared expressly for the occasion; and a motion to rescind the vote of the previous meeting, providing that the papers on the Contemporaries of Burns should not be published, was lost.

On the 4th of June the Club held a meeting and authorized the special committee having charge of the matter to purchase Blackie & Sons' (Glasgow) edition of "The Works of Robert Burns," "The Land of Burns," by the same publishers, and also "Hogg and Motherwell's edition of the Life and Works of Burns."

In consequence of several of the members being about to go into the country for the summer months, the Club resolved to hold its next meeting on the first Wednesday in September, 1851.

Nothing of special importance was transacted at any of the meetings during the fall and winter of 1851, until Dec. 3d, when Wm. A. Weeks, Wm. P. Fetridge, Alexander McGregor, Andrew Weddell, and E. P. Meriam were chosen a committee to superintend the arrangements for the annual festival, and reported progress at a meeting held on January 12th, 1852.

[**1852.**] On Monday, the 26th of January, 1852, (the 25th having fallen on a Sunday,) the Club celebrated the Ninety-Third Anniversary of the Birthday of Burns in the Stackpole House. President William Schouler occupied the Chair, and William Mitchell and William A. Weeks acted as Vice Presidents. Hon. Henry Wilson, President of the Massachusetts Senate, Hon. N. P. Banks, Speaker of the House, Hon. Mayor Seaver of Boston, and other gentlemen of eminence, shared in the hospitality of the Club. The newspapers of the day gave lengthy reports of the speeches, and in point of real intellectual and social enjoyment the meeting had no contemporary rival. Sixty persons joined in the festivities.

At the annual meeting of the Club, held on the 4th day of February, 1852, the committee on the Library reported receipt of Blackie's edition of the Works of Burns, which was placed in the hands of the proprietor of the Club-room, as custodian, until otherwise ordered.

The Treasurer reported that the finances of the Club—all debts being paid—amounted to $35.26.

The following gentlemen were elected officers of the Club for 1852–3 :—

President, . . . WILLIAM SCHOULER.
Vice President, WILLIAM A. WEEKS.
Treasurer, . . . WILLIAM BOGLE.
Secretary, . . . JOHN CHAS. MOORE.

The records of the succeeding months are barren of matters of historical interest, although meetings were regularly held. At this time it became evident that the purposes of the originators of the Club could not be carried out to the extent they had anticipated, and such among their number as had contributed to the literary instruction and amusement of the members failed to attend the meetings, which became more social in their character than had been customary. Valuable additions were made to the library by gift from Wm. P. Fetridge and Wm. A. Weeks.

[1853.] The Annual Burns Festival took place on the 25th of January, 1853, and proved itself an occasion of marked intellectuality and enjoyment.

On the 2nd of February the following gentlemen were chosen officers of the Club, for 1853–4:—

President, . . . William Schouler.
Vice President, William A. Weeks.
Treasurer, . . . William Bogle.
Secretary, . . . John C. Moore.

The record of proceedings during the succeeding year are barren of interest. They, however, show that the Club gradually increased its number of members.

[1854.] At the monthly meeting, held on January 4th, 1854, the Club voted to observe the Ninety-Fifth Anniversary of Burns by a Festival in the Stackpole House, and a committee was appointed to carry out the preparations, consisting of Wm. P. Fetridge, Otis Rich, Edward P. Meriam, Alexander McGregor, John Patterson, William Bogle, and James Anderson.

William A. Weeks presented the Club with a copy of Currie's Edition of the Works of Robert Burns, in four volumes, published in Philadelphia in 1801.

The Anniversary Festival took place in the Stackpole House, when, owing to the departure of the President for Cincinnati, Ohio, the Vice President, Wm. A. Weeks, occupied the Chair. The occasion was one of the most pleasant and gratifying description, and able speeches were made by the President, Mayor J. V. C. Smith, George W. Minns, Judge Thomas Russell, George W. Cooley, John S. Holmes, Frederick O. Prince, William Mitchell, Otis Rich, and others. Sentiment, speech and song kept the meeting harmoniously together until an early hour on the morning of the 26th.

The annual meeting for the choice of officers was held in the Stackpole House on the 4th February, 1854, when the following gentlemen were elected :—

President, . . . WILLIAM A. WEEKS.
Vice President, JOHN C. MOORE.
Treasurer, . . . OTIS RICH.
Secretary, . . . JOHN PATTERSON.

It was unanimously resolved that the Society at each annual meeting hereafter should make choice of a Librarian, and Alexander McGregor was elected.

The Club, on motion of William A. Weeks, seconded by John C. Moore, unanimously adopted the following resolution :—

Resolved, That the thanks of the Boston Burns Club be presented to Col. William Schouler, now of Cincinnati, Ohio, for his long and able services as President of this Club, and for his deep interest in its welfare, and that their best wishes for his prosperity and happiness accompany him to the new scene of his labors.

The Secretary was ordered to transmit a copy of the above resolution to Col. Schouler. A vote of thanks was passed to William Bogle, the retiring Treasurer, and the Secretary ordered to notify him of the same.

The record bears no matter of importance up to the time of the meeting held on the 5th of July, 1854, when Otis Rich, the President *pro tem.*, stated that it was his melancholy duty to announce to the Club the death of the President, William A. Weeks.

A committee was appointed to draft a series of resolutions expressive of the feelings of the Club in consequence of this dispensation of Providence ; and the following were reported by John C. Moore and unanimously adopted :—

WHEREAS, it has pleased Divine Providence, in its inscrutable wisdom, to remove from among us our respected President, Brother and Friend, William A. Weeks, and to deprive his wife and family of a fond husband and father, therefore—

Resolved, That we recognize in this dispensation of the eternal will the warning love of our great Father, and the force of the injunction "be ye also prepared;" and while our hearts mourn the deprivation his family and ourselves have experienced in his loss, we humbly bow beneath the chastening hand of Him who doeth all things for our good.

Resolved, That the manly virtues which characterized the life of our lamented President, his goodness of heart, his modest but exalted talent, and his love for his fellow-men, are features which will always associate themselves with his memory, and incite our imitation.

Resolved, That we sympathize in the spirit of brotherhood with the bereaved wife and family of our departed friend; and that the President furnish them with a copy of these Resolves, which shall be placed on the record of the Club.

John C. Moore, Vice President, resigned his office, as his occupation caused him to reside out of town, and it was accepted. It was agreed to make no present choice of President and Vice President.

At a meeting held on December 6th, the Club voted to hold its annual celebrative Festival, and William Bogle, Alexander McGregor, John Patterson, Lyman T. Vose, Wm. P. Fetridge and William Mitchell were appointed a committee of management.

[1855.] The Annual Birthday Festival took place in the Stackpole House, January 25th, 1855, Otis Rich presiding. Speeches were made from the Chair, and by John S. Tyler, Rev. Mr. Muir, Wm. M. Fleming and James Bennett, tragedians, Judge Russell and others. The occasion was not behind any of its predecessors in the excellent quality of its enjoyments. During the evening, John C. Moore presented the Club, on behalf of a gentleman, whose generosity was not to be published with his name, with a splendid copy of "The Land of Burns," for which the unknown had a hearty vote of thanks.

At the annual meeting, on February 7th, 1855, for the choice of officers, the following gentlemen were unanimously elected:—

President, . . . JOHN S. TYLER.
Vice President, OTIS RICH.

Treasurer, . . . WM. P. FETRIDGE.
Secretary, . . . JOHN PATTERSON.
Librarian, . . . ALEXANDER MCGREGOR.

The Treasurer's report showed a balance on hand, in cash, of $16.61, with no pecuniary responsibilities.

The subject of holding quarterly instead of monthly meetings was discussed at length, but no definite action taken thereon.

From January to December, 1855, it would appear from the Secretary's minutes that no meeting of the Club had been held. On the 22nd of the latter month the Club assembled and voted to hold their annual Celebration of the Birthday of Robert Burns, and the following committee of management was chosen:—Otis Rich, William Bogle, William Mitchell, David Miller and Alexander McGregor. This committee reported in favor of keeping the Festival in the Parker House, and the report was agreed to.

[**1856.**] The annual Festival Meeting, it being the Ninety-Seventh Anniversary of the Birthday of Robert Burns, was held in the Parker House, on Friday evening, 25th January, 1856. The published reports of the proceedings show that it proved itself the most markedly interesting on the record of the Club. President John S. Tyler filled the Chair, and the Vice Presidents were Otis Rich and William Bogle. Excellent speeches were made by the presiding officer, by Hon. George S. Hillard, Mayor Rice, Hon. Chas. A. Phelps, Speaker of the House of Representatives, the Vice Presidents and others. An original poem, written at the grave of Robert Burns, in the churchyard of Dumfries, by Robert Hamilton, formerly of the National Theatre, Boston, was read by William Bogle; and the following witty introduction, and beautiful poem, were read by Dr. Oliver Wendell Holmes, one of the guests on the occasion, and always a cherished friend of the Club:—

I have come with the rest, I can hardly tell why,
With a line I will read you before it is dry;
I know I've no business among you, full well,
But I'm here, notwithstanding, and how, I will tell.

It was not a billet, beginning "Dear Sir;"
No missive like that would have coaxed me to stir;

Nor a ticket, announcing the "on" and the "at,"
And "requesting the honor,"—'twas better than that.

It was done by a visit, from one that you know,
Whose smile is unchilled by life's season of snow,
Whose voice is so winning, resist as you may,
You must do what it says, for it will have its way.

It is true that at first I began to suggest
I should sit like a stranger apart from the rest;
But he said, "To no clan is our banquet confined,
For the heart of the poet belongs to mankind."

Then I timidly asked, "Can I run, at a pinch,
If our friends from the Old World have learned how to lynch?"
For I thought with dismay of the Know-Nothing crew,
And I fancied a yell—"He's a Know-Nothing too!"

I thought of old Porteus, of Hare and of Burke:
I remembered the witches of Alloway Kirk;—
"Why bless you," he said, with a smile, "if you're *cotched*,
You will never be killed, you will only be *Scotched!*

So I came, and I'm here, with a line as I said;
I don't mean the verses that just have been read,
But the ones in my pocket, and so, if you please,
You shall hear them at once if you'll pardon me these.

The mountains glitter in the snow
  A thousand leagues asunder;
Yet here amid the banquet's glow,
  I hear their voice of thunder;
Each giant's ice-bound goblet clinks;—
  A flowing stream is summoned;
Wachusett to Ben Nevis drinks;
  Monadnock to Ben Lomond!

Though years have clipped the eagle's plume
  That crowned the Chieftain's bonnet,
The sun still sees the heather bloom,
  The silver mists lie on it;
With tartan kilt and philibeg,
  What stride was ever bolder
Than his that shewed the naked leg
  Beneath the plaided shoulder?

The echoes sleep on Cheviot's hills
  That heard the bugles blowing,
When down their sides the crimson rills
  With mingled blood were flowing;
The hunts where gallant hearts were game,—
  The slashing on the border,—
The raid that swooped with sword and flame,—
  Give place to "law and order."

Not while the rocking steeples reel
  With midnight tocsins ringing,
Not while the crashing war-notes peal,
  God sets his poets singing;
The bird is silent in the night,
  Or shrieks a cry of warning,
While fluttering round the beacon-light,—
  But hear him greet the morning!

The lark of Scotia's morning sky!
  Whose voice may sing his praises?
With Heaven's own sunlight in his eye,
  He walked among the daisies,
Till through the cloud of fortune's wrong
  He soared to fields of glory;
But left his land her sweetest song
  And earth her saddest story.

'Tis not the forts the builder piles
  That chain the earth together;
The wedded crowns, the sister isles
  Would laugh at such a tether;
The kindling thought, the throbbing words
  That set the pulses beating
Are stronger than the myriad swords
  Of mighty armies meeting.

Thus while within the banquet glows,
  Without the wild winds whistle,
We drink a triple health,—the Rose,
  The Shamrock and the Thistle!
Their blended hues shall never fade
  Till War has hushed his cannon,—
Close-twined as ocean-currents braid
  The Thames, the Clyde, the Shannon!

At a subsequent meeting of the Club, held on the 2d day of February, votes of thanks were unanimously passed to Dr. Holmes and Mr. Hillard for their able contributions to the festival proceedings; also to the President for the very acceptable manner in which he presided on that occasion.

The annual meeting for the choice of officers for 1856–7 was held at the Stackpole House, on February 6th, when the following gentlemen were elected:—

President, . . . JOHN S. TYLER.
Vice President, OTIS RICH.
Treasurer, . . . JOHN L. DIMMOCK.
Secretary, . . . JOHN PATTERSON.

There was no meeting of the Club during the remainder of the year.

[**1857.**] The illness of the President and the Vice-President, at the period of the Annual Birthday Festival, induced the Club to decline its celebration this year.

[**1858.**] The money and bank panic of this year interfered with the intention of the Club to observe its Annual Festival. Beyond making choice of the old officers, no business appears on the record during this year up to nearly its close.

On the 13th of November, a special meeting of the Club was called at the Parker House—the President in the chair—when it was resolved to celebrate the One Hundredth Anniversary of the Birthday of Robert Burns in such style as to make up for the intermissions of the past two years, and the following gentlemen were appointed a Committee of Arrangements:—

John S. Tyler, William Schouler, Otis Rich, William Bogle, William Ellison, Robert I. Burbank, Justin Jones, and John C. Moore. The latter named party was constituted secretary of the committee.

At the special request of the President of the Scots' Charitable Society—Dr. William E. Coale—that its members join the Club in their festivity, the officers of that association were added to the committee of arrangements.

William Bogle was unanimously chosen Treasurer of the Club.

Mr. Ellison, on behalf of Thomas Comer, Esq., leader of the orchestra in the Boston Theatre, presented the Club with an original song, supposed to have been written by James Hogg, "the Ettrick Shepherd," entitled, "The Bonnet and Feather and Claymore," which had been set to music by Mr. Comer, and dedicated by him to the Boston Burns Club. On motion, it was agreed to have the song and music published, with an illustrated title, and Messrs. Bogle, Ellison, and Moore were chosen a special committee to superintend the publication. The Club passed an unanimous vote of thanks to Mr. Comer for his very acceptable gift.

A fac-simile of Burns's manuscript copy of "The Cottar's Saturday Night" was presented to the Club by Mrs. Thomas Inglis, and the grateful thanks of the members tendered to the lady for her valuable gift.

John C. King, sculptor, presented the Club with a copy of his celebrated bust of Burns, to be forwarded as a mark of fraternal regard to the Burns Club of Cincinnati, Ohio, and received the thanks of the members for the same. The President, William Schouler, and William Bogle were appointed a committee to carry out the wish of the donor.

Thirty new members were admitted at this meeting, and thirty-eight members had their names proposed for membership.

The Club held a meeting in the Parker House, on the evening of December 11th, 1858, when thirty-eight new members were admitted.

Justin Jones was unanimously elected Librarian of the Club.

On account of the sickness of the Secretary, John C. Moore was appointed Secretary *pro tem.*

The President, on behalf of the committee of arrangements, reported progress, and produced letters of acceptance of the invitation of the Club to join in the forthcoming festival from several eminent gentlemen.

Mr. Bogle, from the sub-committee appointed for that purpose, reported in favor of the festival being held in the Parker House, and the report was accepted.

At a special meeting of the Club, held on the 28th of December, thirty-six new members were admitted to the Club, and the committee of arrangements made favorable reports relating to the festival proceedings.

[**1859.**] Meetings of the Club were held on the evenings of the 8th and 15th of January, 1859, at which the preparations for the Centennial Festival were further perfected, and thirty-two new members admitted.

The Secretary *pro tem.* presented to the Club an original song—"What's a' the steer makin'?"—written by Benjamin P. Shillaber for the forthcoming festival, which was read, and copies ordered to be printed for members. The thanks of the Club were unanimously voted to Mr. Shillaber for his very acceptable contribution.

The Secretary also reported that he had been notified of the arrival in New York of a box containing presents to the Club, from Miss Isabella Begg, niece of Robert Burns, and from several gentlemen residing in the land of Burns; also a "haggis," made in the Cottage where Burns was born, to be used at the festival.

The following gentlemen were appointed a committee to prepare and publish an abstract history of the Boston Burns Club, with its Constitution and By-Laws, the names of members in full standing, and a full report of the proceedings at the Centennial Festival on the 25th instant: John S. Tyler, William Schouler, John C. Moore, Justin Jones, Z. K. Pangborn, Otis Rich, and John G. Roberts—the committee to have full powers.

Between the 13th of November, 1858, and the 24th of January, 1859, the committee of arrangements held fourteen several meetings for consultation and action. The results of their labors will appear in part from what transpired at the meetings of the Club during the same period, and during the celebration of the Centennial Festival, a full report of which—principally from the *Atlas* and *Bee* of January 26th, 1859—is appended.

CENTENNIAL FESTIVAL

OF THE

BOSTON BURNS CLUB.

JANUARY 25, 1859.

The Centennial Anniversary of the Birthday of Robert Burns was commemorated by the Boston Burns Club this evening, by a banquet at the Parker House. The occasion was one of surpassing and memorable interest, alike for the distinguished gentlemen who honored it by their presence, the great excellence of the literary feast, the cordial spirit that animated the happy gathering, and the profound sentiment of esteem and veneration for the memory of the poet which electrified all hearts. It was worthy of the great poet, of Boston, of the Club which gave it, and of those who were in attendance, and will long be remembered as a truly great festival.

THE HALL AND ITS DECORATIONS.

The hall presented a truly elegant and brilliant appearance. As the eye glanced over table and ornament, and from wall to wall, it met a display of taste and sentiment alike appropriate, suggestive, and beautiful.

At the head of the hall, in rear of the President, and against the wall, was a painting of the monument of Burns on the banks of the Doon, with Alloway Kirk and the Burns cottage in the distance. The painting was executed by John Wilson of Jamaica Plain, an eminent Scottish artist, and a man of superior genius. It was surrounded by a garland of bay leaves; and from the top were suspended garlands of the same material, stretching to either side of the hall.

Below were festoons, and immediately under these a bust of Burns, surmounted by a wreath of fragrant roses and bay leaves. The bust rested upon a fluted pedestal, wreathed with a garland of green. The design was happy and appropriate, and was carried out with success. Upon each side were miniature busts of Sir Walter Scott, General Havelock, General Pellissier, and General Williams, the hero of Kars.

The wall opposite the entrance of the hall was adorned by a painting of Doune Castle, Perthshire, Scotland, also by Wilson, exquisitely done. At the foot of the hall, by the same artist, was a representation of Gibraltar, including a view of the sea. Upon the wall over the entrance was a Gipsey scene by moonlight, the subject being suggested by a passage in Guy Mannering. This, too, was by the hand of Wilson.

In the rear of the Vice-Presidents, inclining upon the wall, were finely-framed photographic pictures, presented to the Club by Mr. David Campbell of Ayr, Scotland, large and splendidly executed, of which the following are the subjects:—

1. The Cottage in which Robert Burns was born, situated about two miles south of the town of Ayr.

2. The Auld Kirk o' Alloway, celebrated as the scene of the witches' dance, in Tam O'Shanter, Auld Clootie's wonderful musical efforts on the Scotch bagpipe, and where

"———Nannie lap and flang
(A souple jade she was and strang),
While Tammie stood, like ane bewitch'd,
And thought his very een enrich'd;
Even Satan glowr'd, and fidg't fu' fain,
And hotch't an' blew wi' might an' main,
Till first ae caper, syne anither,
Tam tint his reason a'thegither
And roars out—'Well done, Cutty Sark!'"

3. The Auld Brig o' Doon, whereon the gray mare Meg of said Tam O'Shanter lost her tail in making good her

retreat from the witches of Kyle unto the less diabolical region of Carrick, on the south side of the Doon.

4. Burns' Monument on the banks of the Doon, in close vicinity to Alloway Kirk and the Auld Brig—the view taken from the south.

A photograph was also exhibited of Mrs. Begg, Burns' sister, who was born June, 1771, and died December, 1858, aged 87½ years. This was executed by D. Campbell, in Ayr, October, 1858, and was a present to the Boston Burns Club from Miss Isabella Begg, a daughter of the venerable lady, along with autographs of the three sons of Robert Burns, and her mother.

Besides the autographs enclosed in Miss Begg's letter, there was an impression of the seal of Robert Burns, now in possession of his grand-daughter, Mrs. Everett, which the poet describes in his letter to Mr. Cunningham, dated "3d March, 1792," as follows: "I am a bit of a herald, and shall give you, *secundem artem*, my arms. On a field, azure, a holly bush, seeded, proper, in base; a shepherd's pipe and crook, saltierwise, also proper, in chief; on a wreath of the colors, a woodlark perching on a sprig of bay tree, proper; for crest, two mottoes, round the top of the crest, *Wood notes wild.* At the bottom of the shield, in the usual place, *Better a wee bush than nae bield.* By the shepherd's pipe and crook I do not mean the nonsense of painters of Arcadia; but a *Stock* and Horn and a *Club.*"

All the above-named mementoes of the bard and his family will be faithfully preserved among the relics of the Boston Burns Club.

In another part of the hall, in a frame, were miniature designs of a cross, Bible, &c., in wood, cut from a branch of Highland Mary's Thorn, at Coilsfield House, Ayrshire, (better known in song as "the Castle o' Montgomery," that being the name of the Eglinton family to whom it belongs,) and obtained by Sanford Howard, June 24, 1858.

In another case were the following specimens:—

Wild flowers from the banks of the Fayle, the scene of the parting of Burns and Highland Mary.

Sweet brier rose from the grounds of Burns' monument.

Purple heath.

Mountain daisy from the field where Burns turned one under with his plough, which gave rise to the poem commencing—

"Wee modest crimson tipped flower."

Grass from the grave of William Burns, the poet's father, in Alloway Kirk yard.

Branch of Mary's Thorn, at Montgomery Castle.

Bird's foot trefoil.

Shamrock trefoil.

All these were collected by Sanford Howard, in June, 1858.

Stereoscopic pictures were exhibited at the tables—the contribution of Mr. Duncan Ballantine, printer, Cumnock, Ayrshire—of Burns' Cottage, the Farmhouse of Mossgiel (two views), the Monument (two views), the Auld Brig, Coobs' Glen (two views), Ballochmyle Viaduct (the scene of the song of "The Lass o' Ballochmyle"), Connar Lynn, and Creswick Glen and the Witches' Stairs, near Sanquhar, Dumfriesshire; also, from Mr. David Campbell of Ayr, two views of Burns' Cottage, with separate groupings of figures, Kirk Alloway, and winter views of the Auld Brig o' Doon and of Burns' Monument on its northern bank.

The Club also received a section of an oak standard used in the original "auld clay biggin" in which Burns first drew the breath of life; also a large portion of Highland Mary's thorn—both of which were partially shown to the guests at the dinner table. These were the gift of Mr. Davison Ritchie, landlord of Burns' Cottage, whose guidwife furnished the haggis for the feast.

Besides these, there were a handsomely-sized billet of "plane-tree" wood, grown in the inside of Alloway's "auld howlet-haunted biggin," the gift of Mr. Hugh Muir, carpenter, at Wrightfield, near the spot where Burns was born, who also forwarded a portion of the iron-work with which the old door of said dilapidated kirk was hung. These the Club will take good care of, there can be little doubt.

The dinner tables, five in number, including the *dais*, which was occupied by the President and the invited guests, were arranged in splendid style, and thousands took advantage of the kindness of Messrs. Parker & Mills, during the day, to inspect their rich and tempting appearance. They were elegantly decorated with flowers and designs wrought in sugar work—among them "Burns' Cottage," "The Monument," a "Scotch Hunting Scene," "Washington's Monument," and a "Temple of Liberty."

GEN. JOHN S. TYLER, President of the Club, occupied the chair at the dinner table; and was assisted by Otis Rich, Vice-President, Justin Jones, Librarian, William Bogle, Treasurer, and Col. Robert I. Burbank, as Vice-Presidents.

At the right of the presiding officer were seated His Excellency, Gov. Banks, Col. Edward G. Parker, one of the Governor's Aids, Hon. Joseph Howe, Hon. Charles A. Phelps, President of the Senate, His Honor Mayor Lincoln, Hon. J. P. Bradlee, President of the Common Council, Peter Harvey, Esq., and others.

On the President's left were seated the Chaplain of the evening, Rev. Mr. Laurie, pastor of the Universalist Church in Charlestown, Ralph Waldo Emerson, Lord Radstock, Hon. George S. Hillard, N. P. Willis, Esq., Dr. Oliver Wendell Holmes, Prof. James Russell Lowell, Capt. Lang, and others.

As soon as the company—which numbered 278—had all entered the hall and stationed themselves around the tables, a blessing was invoked by the Chaplain, and the creature comforts were discussed during nearly two hours. The following bill of fare will show that the appetite would indeed have been a fastidious one which could not find satisfaction at the feast:—

BILL OF FARE.

SOUP.

Mock Turtle. Tomato.

FISH.

Boiled Striped Bass, Hollandaise Sauce. Baked White Fish, Sauce, au Beyrout.

COLD ORNAMENTED DISHES.

Gelatine of Turkey, a la Voliere.
Truffled Duck, in Jelly. Pate de Foie. Gras au Gelee.
Aspic of Oysters, a la Royale. Capon, a la Reine, in Jelly.
Mayonaise of Chicken. Salad of Lobster.
Salad of Scotch Grouse, a la Soyer.

BOILED.

Legs of English Mutton, with Capers.
Capons and Pork, Celery Sauce.
Boston Ham and Tongue.
Turkeys, Oyster Sauce.

ROAST.

Legs of Mutton, Jelly Sauce.
Turkey, Giblet Sauce.
Sirloin of Beef.
Mongrel Geese.

Scotch Pea Fowls, Larded.

ENTREES.

Sweet Breads, with Green Peas.
Lamb Cutlets, a la Marachel.
Fillet of Beef, with Mushrooms.
Pate Chaud, a la Financiere.
Macaroni, en Timbal.
Apple Fritters.

Mutton Kidneys, en Croustade.
Salmi of Quails, with Truffles.
Fillets of Chicken, with Rice.
Venison Cutlets, Jelly Sauce.
Calf's Head, Turtle Sauce.
Escaloped Oysters.

Scotch Haggis, a la "Burns Cottage," and "Cunard."

GAME.

Canvas Back Ducks.
Blue Bill Widgeon.
Black Ducks.
Brandt.

Red Head Ducks,
Mallard Ducks.
Prairie Grouse.
Partridges.

Wild Geese.
Larded Quail.

PASTRY.

Cabinet Pudding, Wine Sauce. Lemon Custard Pudding.
Souffle, a la Vanilla, Charlotte Russe, en Glace.
Madeira Jelly. Italian Cream. Champagne Jelly.
Apple, Mince, Lemon, Cranberry, and Peach Pies.
Meringue Baskets. Chantilli Baskets.
Scotch Holiday Cake.
Confectionary.

DESSERT.

Strawberry Ice Cream. Lemon Ice Cream.
Roman Punch. Orange Sherbet.
Plum Pudding Glace.
Oranges. Apples. Figs. Raisins. Ginger.
Walnuts. Brandy Peaches. Almonds.
Coffee. Olives.

During dinner, and at appropriate intervals thereafter, in response to toasts of a general character, excellent music was furnished by Bell & Baldwin's orchestral band, under the leadership of Mr. Bell.

About half past 7 o'clock, the material repast having come to an end, the intellectual feast was opened by the President, who, as he rose, was received with three hearty cheers, and who spoke as follows :—

SPEECH OF GEN. JOHN S. TYLER.

Gentlemen of the Burns Club :—It is undoubtedly to be regretted by all, and by no one more than myself, that this chair, on this occasion, is not filled by one, better fitted by education, and better qualified by natural ability to discharge the duties of a presiding officer,—at a festival in honor of a poet and man of genius. That I should feel embarrassed, therefore, on rising to discharge the duty imposed by official position—surrounded, as I am, by those, whose learning, eloquence and genius, are conspicuous in the brightest pages of the literature of New England, should be anticipated. That I may keep, however, within the line of safe precedent, permit me to say, in the words of a distinguished gentleman on a late occasion, whose absence we regret, "that the banqueting is ended—but not the *festival*—for *festival* it is." An hundred years ago, this day, in a clay-built cottage on the banks of the Doon, Robert Burns was born. So fragile was the structure, that the first storm of the season destroyed it, and forced his parents to seek shelter in a neighboring house. How unlike the literary structure erected by his genius! This has already survived his natural life more than sixty years, and will endure whilst the human heart responds to the thought—

> "That rank is but the guinea's stamp,
> The man's the gowd for a' that."

Did we need proof of the enduring fame of Burns, we should find it in the existence of such associations as our own, in every land where the language of the Celt and the Anglo-Saxon is spoken—and in the readiness with which the leading poets, orators, and statesmen of each country bring the tributes of their genius, eloquence and wisdom to honor his shrine. It gives me pleasure to state, in this connection, that most of the guests invited by vote of the Club, on this occasion, have accepted our invitation, and now honor our Board with their presence. Among the few who have been compelled to decline, I am sorry to name the Honorable Mr. Everett, from whom I have received the following reply :—

Summer Street, January 22, 1859.

My Dear Sir,—I am extremely indebted to you and Gen. Schouler for your kind invitation, as a Committee of the Boston Burns Club, to attend the celebration of the hundredth anniversary of the birthday of Robert Burns. I leave Boston on the 24th, to fulfil an engagement of a year's standing at Philadelphia, with appointments to speak twice on the way. It will consequently not be in my power to be with you on the 25th, but I shall respond in spirit to every utterance in honor of the great poet, not of Scotland alone, but of all who speak the English tongue, whether in the common dialect, or in that sweet Doric, to which his songs have imparted such an inexpressible charm.

While all you who have Scottish blood in your veins will celebrate the day with emotions of national pride peculiar to yourselves, you will not forbid us, who have learned a higher patriotism from "Scots wha' hae' wi' Wallace bled," a warmer friendship from "Auld Lang Syne," a truer republicanism from "A man's a man for a' that," a deeper reverence for woman from "His 'prentice han' he tried on man," and a more fervid devotion from "The Cottar's Saturday Night," to join with you in doing honor to his memory.

I pray you to admit me to the fellow-citizenship of those who admire, revere and love Burns.

I remain, dear Sir, with friendly salutations and cordial wishes for an agreeable celebration,

Very truly yours, EDWARD EVERETT.

Gen. J. S. Tyler, President of the Boston Burns Club.

I need not say to the members of the Club, that it would have been highly gratifying to us had we been able to solicit the attendance of many other gentlemen, whose literary standing would have rendered their presence desirable and appropriate, but the limited space in this hall, which is as capacious as any in the city suited to the occasion, compelled us to forego our wishes—and I avail myself of this opportunity thus publicly to apologize, in the name of the Club, to every gentleman who may have thought himself neglected.

Your Committee of Arrangements have no occasion, at this stage of the proceedings, to make any report upon the creature comforts provided for your entertainment—this matter has been, as they say in the legislature, laid upon the table—taken up, and ably discussed, to the satisfaction, I trust, of every member. The haggis, made in the cottage of the poet, and that prepared by our esteemed guest, Capt. Lang, are doubtless very good of the kind, and must have been acceptable to the cultivated taste of true Scotchmen—but, I must confess that my own admiration for the national literature of Scotland does not extend to the national cookery. Accompanying the haggis from Ayr, were several articles of interest, kindly contributed by the niece of the Poet, Miss Begg ; Alexander Grant, Esq., proprietor of the Ayrshire Express; Davison Ritchie, Esq. and lady, of Burns' Cottage, Alloway ; Hugh Muir, Esq., of Wrightfield, Alloway ; David Campbell, Esq., of Ayr, and Duncan Ballantine, Esq., of Cumnock, all of which will be carefully preserved in our archives, and produced for the gratification of our successors, at the next Centennial Celebration—at which time, probably, all of us will be forgotten excepting the poets and men of letters who now honor us with their presence, and will live in their works. Having thus alluded to such matters as seemed to demand notice from your President, I purposely forbear to tax your patience with any remarks upon the personal or literary merits of the great bard, in whose honor we have assembled. Of the former, whatever is known has become history. The happiest commentary on his character, perhaps, is from the pen of his kind friend, Mrs. Riddel, who speaks of him as the child of nature and sensibility, unschooled in the rigid precepts of philosophy, and too often unable to control the passions, which proved to him a source of frequent errors and misfortunes, and for which he apologized, in one of his poems, in those lines almost unique for simplicity and beauty :—

"I saw thy pulse's madd'ning play,
Wild send thee pleasure's devious way:
Misled by fancy's meteor ray,
By passion driven:
But yet the light that led astray,
Was light from heaven."

To this it may not be inappropriate to add :—

" Who made the heart, 'tis His alone
Decidedly to try us,
He knows each chord—its various tone,
Each spring—its various bias ;
Then, at the balance, let's be mute,
We never can adjust it ;
What's done, we partly can compute,
But, know not what's resisted."

To speak of the literary character of Burns, I feel my utter incapacity. Happily the affluence of talent around our board renders any effort of the kind as unnecessary as it would be unavailing. Were it otherwise I should be much in the situation of the old lady mentioned by the erudite Joe Miller, whose *first* reason for not loaning her neighbor a washtub, was, that she had none.

I return, therefore, to the line of safe precedent, and proceed "to introduce to you that which remains of our festival—

'The feast of reason and the flow of soul,'

not, of course, to produce this myself, save as mine shall be the hand to touch the rock of Horeb, and unlock the wells of its gushing waters—to usher in the luminaries of speech and of thought."—Kindred spirits grace your table: They wait but the indication of your will, to pour forth in prose and verse, rich tributes of eloquence and genius to the memory of the great poet of nature and humanity, whose birthday we celebrate.

Let us say with Burns, then,—

"Happy we are a' thegither,
Happy we'll be, yin and a',
Time shall see us a' the blyther,
Ere we rise to gang awa'—".

During the above address its sentiments were frequently and heartily applauded, and at its close the President announced Gen. WILLIAM SCHOULER, of the *Atlas* and *Bee*, as the toast-master of the evening, who announced the first toast to be—

1.—*The Memory of Burns.*

The toast was pledged standing, and in silence; after which Mr. GEORGE MOODIE of this city, sang "*The land o' the leal*" with great feeling and effect, the band furnishing an accompaniment; and the assembly manifested its appreciation by marked applause.

The PRESIDENT then said:—" We have with us one who once in his life chose to make an apology, and among the stanzas, I find some words so aptly descriptive of what we all know, that I cannot forbear citing them on this occasion:—

> "Chide me not, laborious band,
> For the idle flowers I brought,
> Every aster in my hand
> Comes home loaded with a thought."

Thus introduced, Mr. Ralph Waldo Emerson rose to respond to the toast of the evening, and was received with loud cheers.

SPEECH OF RALPH WALDO EMERSON.

Mr. President and Gentlemen:—I do not know by what untoward accident it has chanced—and I forbear to inquire—that, in this accomplished circle, it should fall to me, the worst Scotsman of all, to receive your commands, and at the latest hour, too, to respond to the sentiment just offered, and which indeed makes the occasion. But I am told there is no appeal, and I must trust to the inspiration of the theme to make a fitness which does not otherwise exist.

Yet, sir, I heartily feel the singular claims of the occasion. At the first announcement, from I know not whence, that the 25th of January was the hundredth anniversary of the birth of Robert Burns, a sudden consent warmed the great English race, in all its kingdoms, colonies, and states, all over the world, to keep the festival.

We are here to hold our parliament with love and poesy, as men were wont to do in the middle ages. Those famous parliaments might or might not have had more stateliness, and better singers than we—though that is yet to be known—but they could not have better reason.

I can only explain this singular unanimity in a race which rarely acts together, but rather after their watchword, each for himself—by the fact that Robert Burns, the poet of the middle class, represents in the mind of men to-day that great uprising of the middle class against the armed and privileged minorities—that uprising which worked politically in the American and French Revolutions, and which, not in governments so much as in education and in social order, has changed the face of the world.

In order for this destiny, his birth, breeding, and fortune were low. His organic sentiment was absolute independence, and resting, as it should, on a life of labor. No man existed who could look down on him. They that looked into his eyes saw that they might look down the sky as easily. His muse and teaching was common sense, joyful, aggressive, irresistible.

Not Latimer, not Luther, struck more telling blows against false theology than did this brave singer. The "Confession of Augsburg," the "Declaration of Independence," the French "Rights of Man," and the "Marseillaise," are not more weighty documents in the history of freedom than the songs of Burns. His satire has lost none of its edge. His musical arrows yet sing through the air.

He is so substantially a reformer, that I find his grand plain sense in close chain with the greatest masters—Rabelais, Shakspeare in comedy, Cervantes, Butler, and Burns. If I should add another name, I find it only in a living countryman of Burns. He is an exceptional genius. The people who care nothing for literature and poetry care for Burns. It was indifferent—they thought who saw him—whether he wrote verse or not; he could have done anything else as well.

Yet how true a poet is he! And the poet, too, of poor men, of hodden-gray, and the Guernsey-coat, and the blouse. He has given voice to all the experiences of common life; he has endeared the farm-house and cottage, patches and poverty, beans and barley; ale, the poor man's wine; hardship, the fear of debt, the dear society of weans and wife, of brothers and sisters, proud of each other, knowing so few, and finding amends for want and obscurity in books and thought. What a love of nature! and, shall I say it? of middle-class nature. Not great, like Goethe, in the stars, or like Byron, on the ocean, or Moore, in the luxurious East, but in the homely landscape which the poor see around them—bleak leagues of pasture and stubble, ice, and sleet, and rain, and snow-choked brooks; birds, hares, field-mice, thistles, and heather, which he daily knew. How many "Bonny Doons," and "John Anderson my joes," and "Auld Lang Synes," all around the earth, have his verses been applied to! And his love songs still woo and melt the youths and maids; the farm work, the country holiday, the fishing cobble, are still his debtors to-day.

And, as he was thus the poet of the poor, anxious, cheerful, working humanity, so had he the language of low life. He grew up in a rural district, speaking a patois unintelligible to all but natives, and he has made that Lowland Scotch a Doric dialect of fame. It is the only example in history of a language made classic by the genius of a single man. But more than this. He had that secret of genius to draw from the bottom of society the strength of its speech, and astonish the ears of the polite with these artless words, better than art, and filtered of all offence through his beauty. It seemed odious to Luther that the devil should have all the best tunes; he would bring them into the churches; and Burns knew how to take from fairs and gipseys, blacksmiths and drovers, the speech of the market and street, and clothe it with melody.

But I am detaining you too long. The memory of Burns—I am afraid, heaven and earth have taken too good care of it, to leave us anything to say. The west winds are murmuring it. Open the windows behind you, and hearken for the incoming tide, what the waves say of it. The doves perching always on the eaves of the Stone Chapel opposite, may know something about it. Every name in broad Scotland keeps his fame bright. The memory of Burns—every man's, and boy's, and girl's head carries snatches of his songs, and can say them by heart, and, what is strangest of all, never learned them from a book, but from mouth to mouth. The wind whispers them, the birds whistle them, the corn, barley, and bulrushes hoarsely rustle them; nay, the music-boxes at Geneva are framed and toothed to play them; the hand-organs of the Savoyards in all cities repeat them, and the chimes of bells ring them in the spires. They are the property and the solace of mankind.

The wildest cheering followed the conclusion of Mr. Emerson's remarks, a large part of the company rising.

There were loud calls of "More," "Go on." "Go on," and a gentleman rose from one of the tables and said:

"Here are three hundred orators crying out—More!"

The PRESIDENT. Mr. Emerson begs to be excused, not because the well of gushing waters is exhausted, but because, in the kindness of his heart, he thinks that he ought to leave room for gentlemen who are to succeed him.

The second toast was announced—

2. *The Commonwealth of Massachusetts*—Founded by men of Conscience, Courage, Industry, and Truth. Their first duty was to God, their second to Freedom and Humanity, and now—

"They boast a race
To every nobler virtue bred,
And polished grace."

MUSIC—"Hail Columbia."

The PRESIDENT then introduced Governor BANKS as follows. To the second regular toast, we may, with propriety, look for a response from His Excellency the Governor of the Commonwealth. If His Excellency will pardon me for a pun, I will say that in our devotion to the Banks of the Doon, we are unwilling to forget the Banks of our own country. (Great cheering.)

SPEECH OF GOVERNOR BANKS.

MR. PRESIDENT AND GENTLEMEN OF THE BOSTON BURNS CLUB: It is with greater reluctance than any here can conceive, that I rise to respond to the sentiment that has just been uttered; but it is to me a duty which I cannot forbear to perform, however illy it may be done, and whatever grace it may want, and I speak on this occasion only the sentiments that you yourselves and the occasion inspire.

Massachusetts as a Commonwealth owes much to you and yours. The first favor that this ancient Commonwealth ever received, after the blessing of God and the power of the people who first planted their foot upon this ancient and honored colony, was from Scotchmen. I came here, to-night, to present to you, as the representative of our people, my thanks as the representative of those people, for what they did in the hour of our toil and trouble. Though I doubt not it has been presented often to you before—I yet hesitate not to repeat it, for so long as Massachusetts lives, and so long as liberty and learning shall excite a throb in the hearts of the people of this State, our indebtedness and our obligations to the people of Scotland should never be forgotten.

You may remember that when our fathers came here, they were weak in numbers and poor in all but manly spirit. We planted a colony that was designed to give liberty to the world and equal rights to all, and establish in the place of crowns and sceptres the principles of justice and mercy. Our fathers took the continent when it was what they called "bare creation;" but as such it was a prize to them. After eighteen years' struggle, they were arraigned by the crowned power across the great waters. They were told that this theocratic democracy which they had established, where every man was equal to every other man, was not such as the powers of the world ought to recognize, or whose existence should be endured; and they, therefore, summoned the Pilgrim fathers across the waters to answer, by a writ of quo warranto, and show by what right they had undertaken to establish this government. It was the darkest day this colony had ever seen from 1620 up to that hour; and the whole power of Charles the First and his government was summoned and arrayed to crush the New England Commonwealth which had been here established.

It would have been done, sir, for what with the difficulties that surrounded them, the unknown paths of the future, and the heavy cloud that lowered upon them, they had enough to contend with; and had the English government been able to bring its power to bear on this side of the water, though we cannot believe that this Commonwealth would have been destroyed, no man can anticipate or understand what would have been its immediate future. But at that dark moment a light broke from Edinburgh. Charles the First had declared that the liturgy of the Roman missal should be read in Scotland; and the Scotch men and women, and boys and girls, rose up in their might, and, in the language of Burns, they swore that should never be in Scotland. (Loud applause.)

I always respect the religion of Scotland when I remember this fact. It may seem a surprise to us that our political success should have grown out of religious controversy; but it will seem perfectly natural when we remember that in our own Commonwealth no man was then allowed to vote who had not first become a member of the church. (Laughter and applause.) We can refer, in this period of history, to the words of Burns, in which, in 1788, he referred to this country and its future, when he pointed, sir, not with a disposition to pronounce upon the character or the virtues of the American Congress, but to the glorious results of the Revolution through which our people had passed, and the success which even then he saw was destined to crown them, and to predict, in his own glowing language, that the centennial anniversary of their independence would be celebrated with the same spirit and the same enthusiasm with which Scotchmen celebrated their own deliverance from the thraldom of the wrong-headed house of Stuart.

We are indebted, sir, in the Commonwealth of Massachusetts, to the countrymen of Burns on other grounds. Our manufactures, our commerce, our mechanic arts, and our literature have been strengthened, and our success has been enlarged, by the frugal spirit, the untiring energy, and keen, piercing intellect which they at all times and in all directions have given to our industry and practical prosperity. But especially are we indebted to Scotland for the brilliant and heroic spirit, the unsurpassed poetic genius, and the pure love of nature and of the right, which we find in the poetry of Burns—not the poetry for those of scholastic attainments alone, not for one class or another, but for all who wear the form of man, or who can be moved by the highest and purest thoughts which have ever stirred the hearts of the human race in any age of the world. (Prolonged applause.)

I am not disposed, gentlemen, to trespass upon your time, with any disquisition upon his merits as a poet or writer. There are those who can do this better than I, whom you have chosen for this purpose, and so I pass it. But I beg your permission and grace to say, that when you present, on this centennial anniversary of his birth, his character as a man, his genius as a poet, and the spirit of humanity which has immortalized his name, you furnish an example and a philosophy which have warmed the hearts of his fellow-men, and will still strengthen them, so long as human hearts beat within the breasts of men.

From the lowest ranks of life, nerved alone by his own spirit and by his own courage, recognized by none, seeking counsel and support from none, through the strength of his own spirit and the natural brilliancy of his own genius, he achieved for himself an immortality of fame, and gave to the world an illustrious example, which will never cease to be felt. (Cheers.) Sir, if we could give to the people of other lands—to Spain, or to France, or to Russia, or to whatever nation or people you may turn—such words and such lessons, and such power, that should so enter into the hearts of their people as the thrilling melodies of Burns have filled the hearts of Scotchmen, and Englishmen, and Americans, they would hew their way through the thick ranks of privileged orders, and batter down the heavy masses of legislative encroachment, though they were piled mountains high, until they made "Ossa like a wart." (Enthusiastic cheering.)

It was said by the adviser to Charles the First, that in consequence of this outbreak in Scotland, it was necessary that he should allow the colonists of Massachusetts to go on in their own way; and from that period the colonists of Massachusetts have had their own way, and for their own purpose, and have pursued the path of success to which no son of ours this day has other reason to point than as the crowning glory of his race. (Loud applause.)

This is what Burns did for Scotchmen; it is what he has done for Americans; and until years shall cease to roll, and human hearts to beat, there will never be a man, in whatever rank of life you find him, however poor and oppressed, who, with the memory and glory of Robert Burns before him, will not gird and guide himself as if possessed with the spirit and power of truth, of justice, of humanity and right, against whatever odds may be presented. (Loud applause.)

Let me say, then, Mr. President and gentlemen of the Burns Club, taking him as the type of the purpose of Scotland and the Scotch people, and his language as evidence of their power and of their intellect—let me say, in his own words, upon this the hundredth anniversary since God gave him the light of life, and the pen of eloquence, poesy, truth, and power :—

"Auld Scotland has a raucle tongue,
She' just a devil wi' a rung;
An' if she promise old or young
To tak their part,
Tho' by the neck she should be strung,
She'll not desert."

At this point in the proceedings, and at sundry intervals during the evening, Mr. JOHN C. MOORE, the Secretary, announced receipt of telegraphic despatches from kindred Clubs in the United States and Canada. To each and all the Club gave the most fraternal recognition, and prompt replies were made by telegraph. A list of these friendly salutations and sentiments will be found at the close of this report.

Gen. SCHOULER announced the next regular toast as follows :—

3. *The Past lives in the Present*—Upon the veiled Future falls "the light of other days," and with the noisy and discordant tumult of the work-day world, mingles the pleasant music of "Auld Lang Syne." Our venerable and distinguished guest, who unites in his person the experience and wisdom of three generations—HON. JOSIAH QUINCY, SEN.

Mr. JOHN P. ORDWAY's Æolian band sang "*Auld Lang Syne*" in fine style—the company standing, and joining in the choral verses. This was one of the most striking incidents of the evening, and one of the most gratifying tributes to age and worth. As the chorus arose it was taken up outside the hall, and the streets rang with the outpourings of the heart which always accompany the singing of this universal song of friendship.

The PRESIDENT said. Until the last evening, we were assured, at least by our hopes, that the venerable gentleman alluded to in the last toast would favor and honor us with his presence on this occasion. At the last moment, he sent me this note, which I will now read :—

Letter from Josiah Quincy, Sen.

JOHN S. TYLER, Esq., President of the Burns Club:

Dear Sir,—When I accepted your kind invitation to the Burns Centenary Anniversary Dinner, it was under an express reserve that the disabilities incident to old age, relative to an evening convivial meeting, should they occur, would be received as an apology for failing to fulfil my engagement. It will not be necessary for one, approximating his eighty-seventh year, to explain the disabilities which will prevent my presence with you. My desire to unite in your celebration continues intense, but Burns himself has taught me that—

"When life's day is nearly gloamin',
Then farewell vacant, careless roaming,
And farewell cheerful tankards foaming,
And social joys"—

adding, that "prudent, cautious self-control is wisdom's root."

So, wishing you and your assembled associates all the pleasures the occasion promises—above all, that the spirit and genius of your great poet may be present and inspire it—

I am, gratefully,
Your and their obliged servant,
JOSIAH QUINCY.

Boston, January 25, 1859.

The fourth regular toast was then read :—

4. *Pathos and Humor*—Twin sisters of true poetic genius, strikingly illustrated by "Tam O'Shanter," "Hosea Bigelow," and the "Autocrat of the Breakfast Table."

SONG—"Duncan Gray cam here to woo."

The PRESIDENT. I am happy to know that we have a "Boy" with us to-night, who frequently indulges in pathos and humor, and who will say something on this occasion. I introduce to you Dr. OLIVER WENDELL HOLMES.

The "Autocrat" was received with tremendous applause, and proceeded to deliver the following, as his contribution to the dinner-table. In the first line, he made the mistake of calling the date 1857, and was reminded of the error by hearty laughter all round, whereupon he remarked—"Mr. President, I grew two years younger in thinking of this festival."

Poem of Oliver Wendell Holmes.

JANUARY 25TH, 1859.

His birthday.—Nay, we need not speak
  The name each heart is beating,—
Each glistening eye and flushing cheek
  In light and flame repeating!

We come in one tumultuous tide,—
  One surge of wild emotion,—
As crowding through the Frith of Clyde
  Rolls in the western ocean;

As when yon cloudless, quartered moon
  Hangs o'er each storied river,
The swelling breasts of Ayr and Doon
  With sea-green wavelets quiver.

The century shrivels like a scroll—
  The past becomes the present—
And face to face, and soul to soul
  We greet the monarch-peasant.

While Shenstone strained in feeble flights
  With Corydon and Phillis,—
While Wolfe was climbing Abraham's heights
  To snatch the Bourbon lilies,

Who heard the wailing infant's cry,—
  The babe beneath the shieling,
Whose song to-night in every sky
  Will shake earth's starry ceiling—

Whose passion-breathing voice ascends
  And floats like incense o'er us,
Whose ringing lay of friendship blends
  With labor's anvil chorus?

We love him, not for sweetest song,
  Though never tone so tender;
We love him, even in his wrong—
  His wasteful self-surrender.

We praise him, not for gifts divine,—
His muse was born of woman,—
His manhood breathes in every line,—
Was ever heart more human?

We love him, praise him, just for this;
In every form and feature,
Through wealth and want, through wo and bliss,
He saw his fellow-creature!

No soul could sink beneath his love,—
Not even angel blasted;—
No mortal power could soar above
The pride that all outlasted!

Ay! Heaven had set one living man
Beyond the pedant's tether,—
His virtues, frailties, HE may scan,
Who weighs them all together!

I fling my pebble on the cairn
Of him, though dead, undying;
Sweet Nature's nursling, bonniest bairn
Beneath her daisies lying.

The waning suns, the wasting globe,
Shall spare the minstrel's story—
The centuries weave his purple robe,
The mountain-mist of glory!

The company rose and gave the doctor three cheers at the conclusion of his poem.

The fifth toast was then read:—

5. *The Minstrels and Minstrelsy of Scotland*—

"The bonnie bush aboon Traquair,"
"Tweed-side," and "O, I wish I were
Where Helen lies,"
They played in tones which said despair
When beauty dies.

The PRESIDENT. I have to introduce, as one well qualified to discourse of minstrels and minstrelsy, a gentleman who has, on more than one occasion, honored our board with his presence, and who is now, and always will be, a welcome guest. I introduce the Hon. GEORGE S. HILLARD. (Applause.)

SPEECH OF HON. GEORGE S. HILLARD.

A few days since I was asked by a friend if I could tell him why it was that the birthday of Burns is so generally celebrated, both in England and America, and for so long a period had been so. Why is he among so many other poets and men selected for such peculiar honors? The answer to the question does not at once suggest itself, but it can be answered. It is certainly a remarkable fact that, at this moment in all parts of the world, on the banks of the Clyde, the Thames, the Ganges, the St. Lawrence, the Mississippi, Scotchmen, Englishmen, and Americans are met together, to do honor to the memory of a man who was born a hundred years ago this day, in a clay cottage, which his father had built with his own hands,—who made no discoveries in science, or inventions in art; who was not a great soldier or a great statesman, whose birth was humble and whose position through life was obscure, who died young, after having written a few poems, chiefly in the Scottish dialect. He was a singer, and nothing more. He fluttered into the light and warmth of life for a brief season, warbled a few songs, and then disappeared into the grim outer darkness, where no eye could follow his flight. Why is it that he has taken such hold upon the hearts of all who speak with English tongues and read the books of England? Why, among other proofs of this, are we here to-night?

It seems to me that this is due in part to his character as a man, and in part to the peculiar qualities of his poetry. His character was remarkable for its manliness, its sincerity, and its independence. He was too brave for disguises, and too truthful for affectation. In all his life there is no stain of meanness, of treachery, of cowardice, of hypocrisy. If he was vehement in his dislikes, and sometimes almost savage in the expression of them, he was also the most faithful of friends. We mark in him one sure indication of a noble nature—the warmth and constancy of his gratitude. The burden of obligation he wears like a jewel and not like a chain. He often yielded to temptation; but his errors are half atoned for and wholly forgiven by the frankness with which he confesses them. He was born in a very low estate, and reared in bitter, soul-crushing poverty; and this, too, at a time when native worth was less valued, and adventitious distinctions were more regarded than they are now. But in spite of this, his life was marked by a manly independence, sometimes pushed to a fierce and defiant self-assertion. The low-born peasant, whose hands were hardened and whose frame was bent by toil, stood in the presence of noblemen and gentlemen, of wits and scholars, unabashed, "pride in his port, defiance in his eye," as firm upon his feet, as when he strode behind his plough upon the mountain side. He never lowered the flag of genius before the flag of rank. Wherever he met a man's mind, he laid his own alongside of it, yard arm and yard arm, for a fair fight. He respected in others the claims of essential superiority—the God-given patents of nobility—and he exacted from them the same deference. In his life he put into action the sentiment of his fine song:

> Is there, for honest poverty,
>   That hangs his head, and a' that;
> The coward slave, we pass him by,
>   We dare be poor for a' that!
> For a' that, and a' that,
>   Our toil's obscure, and a' that;
> The rank is but the guinea's stamp,
>   The man's the gowd for a' that.

All the primal sympathies of the human soul recognize the power, the charm, of a character of such manly self-reliance, such lofty self-assertion. We follow with admiration the movements of the broad-shouldered, swarthy-cheeked, black-eyed peasant, who on all occasions and in all societies sustains himself with such simple dignity, who plants himself with such assured force on his worth as a man, and whose vigorous, untaught genius beats down the feeble guards of commonplace cultivation and the thin defences of social rank.

There is another winning element in the life of Burns, arising from the fact that he generally acted from impulse, and that his impulses so often led him right. It is a striking remark of Coleridge's, that "motives imply weakness, and the existence of evil and temptation. The angelic nature would act from impulse alone." We may note another illustration of the same truth in the conduct of men and women. Women act more from impulse, and men more from motives. Thus women may make more mistakes than men, but when they do go right their actions have a higher grace, a sweeter flavor. "All men," says Emerson, "love a lover." There is a sympathetic charm in the bearing of one who is visibly and unmistakably under the guidance of a strong and natural emotion. The very follies and extravagances of a man thoroughly in love have a sweet and gracious aspect, and are never ridiculous. The life of Burns glitters with the beauty of fine and cordial impulses. They sometimes hurried him into grave errors, but, as he himself has said, the light that led him astray was light from Heaven. Men who act always deliberately and from well-considered motives—who are always self-vigilant and self-distrustful—who never make mistakes—who never say or do anything they ought not to—may secure esteem, confidence, respect, but rarely inspire love. That we bestow upon characters in which the lights and shades are more strongly contrasted—which sometimes rise above and sometimes fall below the level line of prudence—in which beautiful actions and heroic sacrifices plead for excesses of temperament and the occasional riot of unruly blood; and of these Burns stands forth as the perfect type and representative.

But it is the poetry of Burns, far more than his character as a man, that brings us here to-night. He was a poet of the first order; but that is not all. Among all the poets endowed with a vision and a faculty so high as his, we recall no one whose genius is of so popular a quality. The lowliness of his birth, in some respects a disadvantage, was herein a help to him; for it gave him a comprehension of the common heart and mind of his countrymen, which must have been denied to him had he been born in a higher sphere. Take, for instance, his immortal poem of "The Cottar's Saturday Night." Where can we find another poet with an imagination capable of so idealizing the subject, and yet so familiar with its details as to present a picture as true as it is beautiful? The poetry of Burns hits the heart of man just between wind and water; every line and every word tells. With the inspired eye of genius he looked abroad upon the common life of Scotland; and there found the themes of poetry—and the highest poetry, too—in scenes, in relations, in objects which to the prosaic apprehension seemed compact of hopeless prose. As in works in Florentine mosaic—in which leaves and flowers are reproduced in precious stones—our pleasure is made up in part from the beauty of the material used, and in part from the familiar character of the forms represented, so in reading the poetry of Burns, we are not only charmed with the genius it displays, but thrilled with a strange electric delight in seeing the ordinary themes of every-day life so glorified and transfigured. At his touch, the heather bloom becomes an amethyst, and the holly leaf turns into emerald. Every man can comprehend, feel, and enjoy the poetry of Burns; for this no other training is needed than the training of life. There are no learned allusions, no recondite lore, no speculations that transcend the range of average experience. To have seen the daisy blow and heard the lark sing—to have clasped the hand of man and kissed the lips of woman—are preparation enough for all that he has written. The sentiments with which the poor man reads him are compounded, perhaps unconsciously, of admiration and gratitude—gratitude to the genius which has poured such ideal light around this common earth—which has empurpled with celestial roses the very turf beneath his feet—which has opened to him, the child of poverty and toil, the fairy world of imagination—which has held to his lips the sparkling elixir, the divine nepenthe, of poetry—which on its mighty wings has soared with him into regions where he could see the waving of angelic robes and hear the music of paradise!

The genius of Burns expressed itself most naturally and easily in that shape which is best adapted for popular influence. His songs are his best, his most characteristic poems; and in all British literature he is the first of song-writers. A song, as it is the airiest, the most subtle, the most delicate form in which the conceptions of a poet are embodied, so it is the most volatile, the most lightly borne, the most easily diffused. A song has wings but no feet: it darts from lip to lip, and from heart to heart. The empire of a great epic or didactic poet may be higher, but that of a great song-writer is wider. The reason of this is that a song is the growth of that part of our nature in which all men are alike. A good song may be defined to be one man's music and every man's experience.

The themes of the song-writer are taken from the passions, the emotions, the sentiments of the common heart. They are found blooming by the side of that great highway on which humanity travels from the cradle to the grave. The mere literary merit of the songs of Burns can hardly be overstated, but their highest charm comes from their truth. Every line in them is vital; there is none of the cold and glittering beauty of frost work; they spring not from the cunning brain, but from the beating heart. There are many songs in the English language—and good songs, too—in which we can plainly see the marks of elaboration—the lines of the graving and chasing tools. But the songs of Burns are growths and not manufactures; as the fountain gushes from the earth—as the daisy springs from the sod—so they have sung themselves. The metre was but the mould into which the liquid heart was poured. We cannot conceive of a word in them ever having been any other than it is.

The greater part of the songs of Burns are love songs; and herein the life of the man is reproduced in his verse. Burns was always a lover; his temperament was so ardent and susceptible that he never saw a fine female face without falling in love with it. Love was with him no mystical sentiment, no etherial tenderness, no airy rapture; it was not of that class of which some sublimated philosopher says that it is born with the first sigh and dies with the first kiss; but it was a passionate flame which ran like lightning through his veins, felt in the heart, felt in the pulse. His love poetry is informed with burning life; his love songs are the foam-flakes of a heaving sea of fire. This element of truth it owes to the fact that it was invariably the utterance of emotions actually felt. He wrote not from general imaginations, but from particular impressions. He had ever before him, in his mind's eye, some individual face or form—some Jean Armor, Mary Morrison, or Jessie Lewars—to inspire his muse. His biographers will tell you to whom belonged the rosy lips, the snowy bosoms, the golden ringlets, the "twa lovely een of bonnie blue," that are immortalized in his verses. Alas, where are they now? The love poetry of Burns is also nearly as remarkable for its purity, its tenderness and sweetness, as for its passionateness and truth. He sometimes offends against decorum in his poems, but almost never in his songs.

Burns is thus the laureat of love. He is the best interpreter of that universal passion—that great magician under whose sway all men are, or have been, or are to be. Hence one chief ingredient in his popularity and power. His love poetry addresses the experiences or the recollections of all. Fervid is the noonday glow of love—pensive and sweet are its twilight memories. The old man, whose pulse has long been calm, will read with delight the songs of Burns, for they recall and renew those delicious days when a white frock and a pink sash were all that were wanted to make an angel of.

But the highest charm of Burns' poetry is one which his countrymen alone can feel in its full extent, and that is its intense nationality. Scotland had had before him philosophers and men of letters of the first class; like Robertson, Adam Smith, David Hume, Dugald Stewart, and Thomas Reid, novelists like Smollett, poets like Thomson and John Home; but, as Carlyle truly remarked, there was nothing in them that was Scottish, nothing that was indigenous. They did honor to Scotland, but they did nothing to make the peculiar characteristics of Scottish life and manners known to the world. There had also been writers imbued with this national flavor, like Ferguson and Allan Ramsay; but they were not first-class men. Burns was the first man who, with a genius of the highest order, found his inspiration and his themes upon the soil of his native land. He was a great poet and a national poet too. In his dedication of the Edinburgh edition of his poems to the noblemen and gentlemen of the Caledonian hunt, he says—"The poetic genius of my country found me, as the prophetic bard Elijah did Elisha—at the plough, and threw her inspiring mantle over me. She bade me sing the loves, the joys, the rural scenes and rural pleasures of my native soil in my native tongue." This is said with as much truth as beauty. Burns is a thorough

Scotchman—the flavor of the soil can be tasted in everything he wrote. He was himself perfectly conscious of this feeling; he knew where his strength lay.

> The rough bur-thistle spreading wide
> Among the bearded bear—
> I turned the weeder-clips aside
> And spared the symbol dear.

The thistle was to him not a weed but a symbol: the poet spared what the farmer should have cut down. When we add to this that he has sung in vigorous and animated verse the praises of a haggis, it must be admitted that the force of nationality can no farther go. We outside barbarians admire the poetry of Burns heartily and honestly: we may flatter ourselves that we feel all its power and are thrilled by all its music: but beyond all question we are mistaken. There is an inner circle of apprehension and comprehension into which we cannot enter, into which no one can enter but he who has learned upon a mother's knee that sweet and expressive dialect which he used with such grace and such power.

Men of Scotland! countrymen of Burns! you do well to celebrate his memory with song and speech, with eyes suffused, and hand clasped in hand. You owe him a debt of gratitude which you can never repay. You are wiser than your fathers. God sent them this glorious genius, and they made him an exciseman, with seventy pounds a year, and allowed some paltry jack-in-office to tell him that his business was to act, not to think. Alas! the pity of it! the pity of it! He has long been where cruel indignation can no longer lacerate his heart. You can only pour your vain libations upon his dust. This will not profit him, but it will profit you. You have a right to thank God in your prayers for the gift of Burns. Every Scotchman has a right to hold up his head higher from the fact that Burns was his countryman. For him every blue-eyed lassie that runs about your flowery braes, or bathes her feet in the wimpling burn, is a fairer object. For him every heathery hill glows in richer purple; every glen lies steeped in softer light; every mountain lake gleams with deeper blue. For him the wild rose burns with finer flame, and the thorn exhales a sweeter breath. His spirit hangs like a glory over your land; your streams are vocal with his name: the lyric lark sings of him whose music was sweeter than his own: of him your torrents rave: your winds murmur of him. The Scotland that he left was not the Scotland that he found. By him it was exalted, glorified, idealized; by him it was bathed in light that never shone on earth or sea—and until the rocks around your coast shall melt in the sun—until your hills shall pass away like the vapors that curl and play upon their sides, let not his image be banished from your hearts, let not his praise be silent on your lips.

Mr. Hillard's address, as it properly deserved, was applauded to the echo. Among the admirers of Burns none has a higher place than Mr. Hillard, and no one among us has done more than he, in association with the Boston Burns Club, to give its annual celebrations the high literary repute they always have had.

The next toast was read as follows:—

6. *The Poets and Poetry of America*—"How beautiful upon the mountains are the feet of him that bringeth good tidings, and that publisheth peace." "The wilderness and the solitary place shall be glad for them, and the desert shall rejoice and blossom as the rose."

Mr. Moody here sung the following song—(composed, by request of the Secretary, for the occasion,) to the tune of "What's a' the steer, Kimmer"—a famed old Jacobite lay of the "auld forty-five:"

Song, Composed by Benj. P. Shillaber.

What's a' the steer makin'! What's a' the steer?
The Peasant Bard first saw the light this day a hunder year;
An' a' our hearts expand, blythely—a' our hearts expand
Wi' honor o' his name that's known in every land;
  For 'twas a blessed thing, surely, 'twas a blessed thing,
  Sin' a' the world was better for't when Burns began to sing;
  Sae we'll raise our voices high, in tones of grandest cheer,
  That Rob the Rhymer saw the light this day a hunder year!

His fame's brawly won, nei'bor, his fame's brawly won,
An' a' the lan's unite to crown auld Scotia's gifted son;
They plait a laurel wreath for him—his weel achievit bays—
And bring rich gifts o' mind as tributes to his praise;

For though o' humble birth, nei'bor, tho' o' humble birth,
His genius gied him station wi' gentles o' the earth;
Sae we're a' unco happy, and we'll mak' a joyfu' steer,
Sin' ROB THE POET saw the light this day a hunder year.

The humble and the high, nei'bor, the humble and the high,
Combine to glorify the bard whose song will never die,
In every clime 'tis heard wi' joy—in every gentle hame—
An' sparkling een grow brighter at mention o' his name:
Oh he's the puir man's friend! nei'bor, he's the puir man's friend,
An' hodden gray tak's rank, where worth its grace doth lend,
There's a blessin' on the hour that hauds us captive here,
For ROB THE PUIR MAN'S BARD saw light this day a hunder year!

Wide is his kin spreadin', wide is his clan,
They're found wherever men most nobly act the man;
Not where the tartans gleam, nor yet the bonnets blue,
But where the heart is tender, and men are leal an' true.
'Tis nae tie o' bluid, nei'bor, nae tie o' bluid—
His sangs unite the nations, in ae braid britherhood;
Sae honor crown the time, and pang it fu' o' cheer,
Sin' BURNS THE PLOUGHMAN BARD was born this day a hunder year.

A united call for a repetition of this beautiful song was responded to by Mr. Moodie, and the succeeding applause was most liberal and hearty.

The PRESIDENT. The toast just now announced—if you have not forgotten it in admiration of the song which followed—was "The Poets and Poetry of America." Among those who have added largely to the poetry of which our nation is proud, there is one who has written the following lines:—

"He spoke of Burns: men rude and rough
Pressed round to hear the praise of one
Whose heart was made of manly, simple stuff,
As homespun as their own.

"In his broad breast, the feeling deep
That struggled on the many's tongue,
Swells to a tide of thought, whose surges leap
O'er the weak thrones of wrong."

Gentlemen, I have the pleasure of introducing to you JAMES RUSSELL LOWELL, Esq.

Mr. LOWELL said—I come here tonight double-barrelled, with a piece about seven minutes long and one about two minutes and a half long. Which will you have? (Cries of "both, both.") Well, I'll give you the long one first. And if you think me a little free, I beg you to remember that what I read is based on a Scotch ballad, of which the one whose birthday we celebrate was fond: and besides, I am a son of a clergyman who was educated in Edinburgh, and from whose principles I hope I have not departed. (Laughter.) I desire to say that I feel keenly the advantages—the disadvantages, and then the advantages—of my position here as junior: almost everything that I have to say has already been said, but I have the best chance of anybody that has yet spoken to see the next centennial. (Laughter.)

Poem of James Russell Lowell, Esq.

I.

A hundred years! they're quickly fled,
  With all their joy and sorrow,
Their dead leaves shed upon the dead
  Their fresh ones sprung by morrow;
And still the patient seasons bring
  Their change of sun and shadow,
New birds still sing with every spring,
  New violets spot the meadow.

II.

A hundred years! and Nature's powers
  No greater grown nor lessened!
They saw no flowers more sweet than ours,
  No fairer new moon's crescent;—
If she would treat us poets so,
  Would so from winter free us,
And set our slow old sap aflow
  To sprout in fresh ideas!

III.

Alas! I think, what worth or parts
  Have brought me here competing,
To speak what starts in myriad hearts
  With Burns's memory beating;
A theme like this would Bryant choose,
  Longfellow, Holmes or Whittier;
If my poor muse can't fill their shoes,
  Pray pardon her and pity her.

IV.

As I sat musing what to say
And how my verse to number,
Some elf in play passed by that way
And sank my lids in slumber;
And on my sleep a vision stole
Which I will put in metre,
Of Burns's soul at the wicket-hole
Where sits the good St. Peter.

V.

The saint, methought, had left his post
That day to Holy Willie,
Who swore, "Each ghost that comes shall toast
In brimstone, will he, nil he;
There's nane need hope with phrases fine
Their score to wipe a sin frae;—
I'll chalk a sign, to save their tryin'—
A hand ☞ *Vide infra!*"

VI.

Alas! no soil's too cold or dry
For spiritual small potatoes,
Scrimped nature's spry the trade to ply
Of *diaboli advocatus*,
Who lay bent pins in the penance stool
Where Mercy spreads a cushion,
Who've just one rule for knave or fool,
It saves so much confusion.

VII.

So, when Burns knocked, Will knit his brows,
His window-gap made scanter,
And said, "Go rouse the other house,
We lodge no Tam O'Shanter!"
"*We* lodge!" laughed Burns, "now well I see
Death cannot kill old nature,
No human flea but thinks that he
May speak for his Creator!

VIII.

"But Willie, friend, don't turn me forth,
Auld Clootie needs no gauger,
And if on earth I had small worth,
You've let in worse, I'se wager!"
"Na, nane has knockit at the yett
But found me hard as whunstane,
There's chances yet your bread to get
Wi Auld Nick, gaugin' brunstane."

IX.

Meanwhile the 'Unco' Guid' had ta'en
  Its place to watch the process,
Flattening in vain on many a pane
  Their disembodied noses;
Remember, please, 'tis all a dream,
  One can't control the fancies
Through sleep, that stream with wayward gleam
  Like midnight's boreal dances.

X.

Old Willie's tone grew sharp's a knife;
  "*Imprimis*, I indict ye
For makin' strife wi' the water o' life
  And preferrin' *aqua vitæ*."
Then roared a voice with lusty din,
  Like a skipper's when 'tis blowy,
"If *that's* a sin, *I'd* ne'er ha' got in,
  As sure's as my name is Noah!"

XI.

Sly Willie turned another leaf,—
  "There's many here ha'e heard ye,
To the pain and grief o' true belief,
  Say hard things o' the clergy!"
Then rang a clear tone over all,—
  "One plea for him allow me,
I once heard call from o'er me, 'Saul,
  Why persecutest thou me?'"

XII.

To the next charge vexed Willie turned
  And, sighing, wiped his glasses,—
"I'm much concerned to find ye yearned
  O'er warmly tow'rd the lasses!"
But David cried, "Your ledger shut,
  E'en Adam fell by woman,
And hearts close shut with if and but,
  If safe, are not so human!"

XIII.

When sudden glory round me broke
  And low melodious surges,
Of wings whose stroke to splendor woke
  Creation's farthest verges;
A cross stretched, ladderlike, secure
  From earth to heaven's own portal,
Whereby God's poor, with footing sure,
  Climbed up to peace immortal.

XIV.

I heard a voice serene and low,
  (With my heart I seemed to hear it,)
Fall soft and slow as snow on snow
  Like grace of the heavenly spirit;
As sweet as over new-born son
  The croon of new-made mother,
The voice begun, "sore-tempted one!"
  Then, pausing, sighed, "our brother!"

XV.

"If not a sparrow falls, unless
  The Father sees and knows it,
Think! recks He less His form express?
  The soul His own deposit?
If only dear to Him the strong
  That never trip nor wander,
Where were the throng whose morning song
  Thrills His blue arches yonder?

XVI.

"Do souls alone clear-eyed, strong-kneed,
  To Him true service render.
And they who need His hand to lead,
  Find they His heart untender?
Through all your various ranks and fates,
  He opens doors to duty,
And he that waits there at your gates
  Was servant of His Beauty.

XVII.

"The earth must richer sap secrete
  (In time, could ye but know it!)
Must juice concrete with fiercer heat
  Ere she can make her poet;
These larger hearts must feel the rolls
  Of stormier-waved temptation,
These star-wide souls between their poles
  Bear zones of tropic passion.

XVIII.

"Her cheaper broods in palaces
  She raises under glasses,
But souls like these, heaven's hostages,
  Spring shelterless as grasses;
He lov'd much! that is gospel good,
  Howe'er the text you handle;
From common wood the cross was hewed,
  By love turned priceless sandal.

XIX.

"If scant his service at the kirk
He *paters* heard and *aves*
From choirs that lurk in hedge and birk
From blackbird and from mavis;
The cowering mouse, poor unroofed thing,
In him found mercy's angel,
The daisy's ring, brought every spring,
To him Faith's fresh evangel!

XX.

"Not he the threatening texts who deals
Is highest 'mong the preachers,
But he who feels the woes and weals
Of all God's wandering creatures;
He doth good work whose heart can find
The spirit 'neath the letter;
Who makes his kind of happier mind,
Leaves wiser men and better.

XXI.

"They make Religion be abhorred
Who round with darkness gulf her,
And think no word can please the Lord
Unless it smell of sulphur;
Dear Poet-heart, that childlike guessed
The Father's loving-kindness,
Come now to rest! thou didst His hest,
If haply 'twas in blindness!"

XXII.

Then leapt Heaven's portals wide apart,
And, at their golden thunder,
With sudden start I woke, my heart
Still throbbing full of wonder;
"Father," I said, "'tis known to Thee
How thou thy Saints preparest,
But this I see—Saint Charity
Is still the first and fairest!"

XXXIII.

Dear Bard and Brother! let who may
Against thy faults be railing!
(Though far, I pray, from us be they
That never knew a failing!)
One toast I'll give, and that not long,
Which thou would'st pledge if present,—
To him whose song, in nature strong,
Makes man of prince and peasant!

The applause which frequently interrupted the recitation of Mr. Lowell's fine poem showed a high appreciation of its beauties.

Being called upon, unanimously, to favor the Club with the shorter poem mentioned, Mr. Lowell complied, and, in doing so, ministered greatly to the hilarity of the hour. The Committee on Publication regret their inability to furnish this characteristic production of Mr. Lowell's muse.

[Had the time favored its introduction here, SIDNEY WEBSTER, Esq., who had it in his possession, would have presented an autograph letter of Robert Burns, written by him for a friend to send to the *Morning Chronicle*. The history of the letter in question is as follows:—A neighbor of the poet's at Dumfries called on him and complained that he was greatly disappointed in the irregular delivery of the *Chronicle*. Burns said, "Why do not you write to the editors of the paper?" The reply was, "Good God, sir, can *I* presume to write to the learned editors of a newspaper?" "Well," said Burns, "if *you* are afraid of writing to them *I* am not; and, if you think proper, I'll draw up a sketch of a letter which you may copy." Burns tore a leaf from his excise book and produced the sketch, which his friend took home to transcribe; but the caution the enemies of Burns had taught him to exercise prompted him to beg a friend to wait on the person for whom it was written and request that it should be returned. The request was complied with, and the letter was not printed until after the poet's death, when it appeared in his works, and may be found among his correspondence.]

The PRESIDENT. Gentlemen, among the bards of New England invited to grace your board this evening, is one whose presence we miss, and the cause of whose absence we all regret. I allude to the Quaker poet, JOHN GREENLEAF WHITTIER. [Applause.]

In his necessary absence, caused by indisposition, he has kindly transmitted to us some lines, which will doubtless afford you all great pleasure. In alluding to him, permit me to recall to your minds a verse from one of his poems, aptly descriptive of one trait in the character of Burns. He writes thus:

"Sworn foe of cant, he smote it down,
  With trenchant wit unsparing,
And, mocking, rent with ruthless hand,
  The robe pretence was wearing."

Mr. Emerson will have the kindness to read the production of Mr. Whittier. [Applause.]

John G. Whittier's Letter and Poem.

Amesbury, 22*d* 1*st mo.*, 1859.

DEAR FRIEND: I gratefully acknowledge, through thee, the invitation to the celebration of the centennial anniversary of the birthday of the poet whom I have long regarded as the truest and sweetest of all who have ever sung of home, and love, and humanity.

As I may not be able to be with you, I venture to offer a few lines, which, however inadequate to the occasion, attest a sincere tribute to the great World Singer.

Very truly thy friend, JOHN G. WHITTIER.

JOHN S. TYLER, Esq., President of Boston Burns Club.

How sweetly come the holy psalms
  From saints and martyrs down,
The waving of triumphal palms
  Above the thorny crown!
The choral praise, the chanted prayers
  From harps by angels strung,
The hunted Cameron's mountain airs,
  The hymns that Luther sung!

Yet, jarring not the heavenly notes,
  The sounds of earth are heard,
As through the open minster floats
  The song of breeze and bird!
Not less the wonder of the sky
  That daisies bloom below;
The brook sings on, though loud and high
  The cloudy organs blow!

And, if the tender ear be jarred
  That, haply, hears by turns
The saintly harp of Olney's bard,
  The pastoral pipe of Burns,
No discord mars His perfect plan
  Who gave them both a tongue,
For he who sings the love of man
  The love of God hath sung!

To-day be every fault forgiven
  Of him in whom we joy;
We take, with thanks, the gold of heaven
  And leave the earth's alloy.
Be ours his music as of Spring,
  His sweetness as of flowers,
The songs the bard himself might sing
  In holier ears than ours.

Sweet airs of love and home, the hum
  Of household melodies,
Come, singing, as the robins come
  To sing in door-yard trees.
While heart to heart, two nations lean
  No rival wreaths to twine,
But, blending in eternal green,
  The holly and the pine!

Mr. Whittier's poem had a rapturous reception, each sentiment being the signal for applause.

7. *Scotland*—A speck upon the earth's surface, "a land of brown heath and shaggy wood"—the writings of her philosophers and metaphysicians, her historians and novelists, her moralists and divines, are read of all men, and the songs of her poets and the music of her minstrels reverberate in unbroken harmony around the world.

Mr. KELLY, of "Ordway's Æolians," sang the following original song—the music by Thomas Comer, Esq.—which was heartily applauded. It is dedicated to the Boston Burns Club. (See page 22.)

The Bonnet and Feather and Claymore.

Hurrah for the lad! that, wi' heart and wi' hand,
Will fight for his lassie, his freedom and land,
And who for auld Scotia will gallantly stand,
    Wi' his Bonnet and Feather and Claymore!

His brows I will deck wi' the bold eagle's wing,
And the tartan around his braid shoulders I'll fling,
And the name o' my sodger wi' rapture I'll sing—
    His Bonnet and Feather and Claymore!

The tradesman gi'es claes and the ploughman gi'es food,
And the statesman he toils for his country's gude;
But the sodger protects a' their rights wi' his blude—
    His Bonnet and Feather and Claymore!

And when the war-din o' the foe rattles nigh,
His heart, like his banner, is fluttering high;
For his country and freedom he'll conquer or die,
    Wi' his Bonnet and Feather and Claymore!

Hurrah for the lad! that, wi' heart and wi' hand,
Will fight for his lassie, his freedom and land;
And who for auld Scotia will gallantly stand,
Wi' his Bonnet and Feather and Claymore!

[This song, with its beautifully appropriate music, has been published by Messrs. Russell & Tolman, 291 Washington Street, Boston. It has a finely illustrated title and dedication.]

The PRESIDENT. Gentlemen, it was within the scope of our arrangements to ask from the Hon. ROBERT C. WINTHROP a response to the sentiment just given. Until this day, Mr. Winthrop, who has taken much interest in this occasion, had assured me, with but slight expression of doubt, that he would be with us; but circumstances prevented. I now read you a note received from him this afternoon :—

Letter from Hon. Robert C. Winthrop.

Boston, January 25, 1859.

GEN. JOHN S. TYLER, President, &c. :—

My Dear Sir,—You may not have forgotten that, in acknowledging the invitation of the Burns Club, many weeks ago, I suggested a doubt whether it would be in my power to attend their festival this evening. Finding myself constrained to-day to abandon the idea of being with you, I can only thank you for remembering me so kindly among your honored guests, and offer you my best wishes for the success of the occasion.

In commemorating the Patriot Bard, whose song has shed such a glory over his native land, and to the brilliancy of whose genius every tongue and every heart at your table will bear witness, you will not fail to recall, also, some of the other worthies of the same classic soil.

The world's debt to Scotland, not merely for song and for story, but for not a few of the noblest illustrations of science and of art, of philosophy and of philanthropy, can hardly be over-estimated. From the days of that illustrious Napier of Merchistoun, of whom the historian Hume did not hesitate to say that he was the person to whom the title of *a great man* is more justly due than to any other whom his country has ever produced, and whose name has been so agreeably revived among us of late by the genial and accomplished Minister of Great Britain at Washington—down to the more recent period of Walter Scott and Thomas Chalmers and Hugh Miller—Scotland has rarely if ever been without a son to delight, instruct and elevate the human soul.

Nor can I forget that New England owes to the land of Burns the earliest example of an organized Association of Benevolence—the

Scots' Charitable Society dating back its original institution to the year 1658.

Allow me, in reference to this interesting historical fact, to offer you the subjoined sentiment,

And believe me, dear Sir,
Respectfully and truly,
Your obliged and obedient servant,
ROBERT C. WINTHROP.

The Scots in New England Two Hundred Years Ago—They proved themselves worthy forerunners of the immortal Bard, who said—

But deep this truth impressed my mind—
Through all His Works abroad,
The heart benevolent and kind
The most resembles God.

After due honor had been done to Mr. Winthrop's sentiment the PRESIDENT said :—In the absence of the distinguished gentleman whose letter I have just read, I am happy to say, that, although Auld Scotia herself is not responsive, we have no difficulty in finding out *Howe* we shall act, for Nova Scotia is well represented. I have the honor to introduce to you the Hon. JOSEPH HOWE of Nova Scotia. (Cheers.)

Speech of HON. JOSEPH HOWE, of Halifax, N. S.

MR. CHAIRMAN AND GENTLEMEN :—We were under the impression in the British Provinces that this was the land of steady habits, but I am prepared to testify that I landed here on the second of July, and I found all Boston eating and drinking ; and I am about to depart from your shores to-morrow morning, and I leave you eating and drinking still. (Laughter.) I am called upon to respond to a toast to which the Hon. Mr. Winthrop should have responded. Hyperion to the Mummy! If upon short notice I appear before you unprepared, all I can say to you is, that I have the excuse of the Irishman, who, when he saw men all around him armed with double-barrelled guns and nine-barrelled revolvers, shook his shillelah, and said—" Here goes for the instrument that never misses fire." (Laughter.)

Mr. Chairman, I know that the men of Boston consider us in the Eastern Provinces as outside barbarians. I know that we are looked upon as the territories that have not been admitted into the American Union; and that we are considered as people who have not a reason to give for the faith that is in us; and yet, I am called upon, of a sudden, to represent all North America; and what is more and what is worse, all Scotland beside! Well now, as regards Scotland, I think she can speak for herself. (Applause.) She can speak for herself in every department of intellectual exertion; in history, through her Humes and her Robertsons; in modern history, through her Carlyles; in poetry, through her Burns, her Ramsay and her Scott; and in metaphysics as well. Look at her exertions in modern warfare. Think of that single red line of Highland tartans at the battle of Balaclava. (Applause.) That single but indomitable line turned back the entire army of autocratic Russia. In any department she can speak for herself. But I am not a Scotchman, gentlemen. I have the misfortune to have been born of a New England man in the far-off Province of Nova Scotia. It has been my fortune to be born of a bad stock in a bad country. (Laughter.) But I can say this, that while I am bound by the limitation of the toast to exalt old Scotland, I cannot help exalting Nova Scotia, which is New Scotland, on this side of the Atlantic. It is true, that in looking to the recent struggles which illustrate the history of our country, we find that Sir Colin Campbell, a warrior of your race, your blood, your language, your literature, headed the army that marched upon Lucknow; but there he found little Jack Inglis, a countryman of my own, a boy that I knew at school, defending that noble position, and upholding the honor of his race and the glory of his country. (Applause.)

Now, my friends, I am a stranger, but I ask your indulgence, your friendship. (Voices—"you have it!") But there is one man here of whom I would almost ask your condemnation, for he once put me in bodily fear by calling on me for a speech in Faneuil Hall. I shall never forget my sensations when I was so suddenly called upon to address 1500 Americans. Yet to-night, I am almost entirely dumbfounded; for on one side is a most estimable Mayor, on the other a most excellent Governor, and I am in the presence of an "Autocrat" beside, and being a simple man "from the Provinces," you can imagine how I feel. (Laughter.)

But, after all, what are we here for? We are here to feel the eloquence of the hour and of the occasion, and do deeper honor to Robert Burns. And what does he teach us? He teaches us that "one touch of *nature* makes the world kin." He teaches us, wherever we live, to exclude from our literary system, from our legal system, every badge of servitude; so to rear our offspring on the American Continent that, from Vancouver's Island to Halifax, a man shall be a man for a' that. The preachers tell us, (and among your preachers allow me to say with what infinite delight I have listened to Henry Ward Beecher in New York,) your preachers tell us to make our application of the lesson of the day. And why are we met to-day? Is it to scatter flowers upon the grave of Burns? No, sir; it is to profit by his example, to treasure his precepts, till they may pervade this Continent, from end to end.

But I will depart from this broad view of the question, and give you a single illustration of the power of the poet Burns. I do remember a boy of twelve years of age, wild, reckless, given to shooting wild ducks, to playing at marbles and base ball; and I remember the day on which, throwing himself down, lazily and listlessly, upon the sofa, his sister, but a year and a half older, read to him Burns' "Cottar's Saturday Night." And on that day in that boy's soul was born a love of poetry and literature; and in less than a month after he heard the "Cottar's Saturday Night," he lay upon his sleepless couch and read that and all other of Burns' poems, and devoured them; and he grew up a lover of poetry and literature. And that boy's sister died far off upon the distant seas, and was buried in a foreign land. He knows not her grave, but he respects her memory; and years after, it so happened that, sent upon public business from his native province, that boy went to old Scotland, and lingered for a day or two in the vale of Nith. He saw the beautiful stream winding through the valleys there, and the very description of black cattle that Burns had bought and sold, brought into the market; he saw the very peasantry among whom Burns had mingled, and at the very tavern he sat, where Burns had smoked and laughed and drunk. And the sexton took him into the grave-yard, where he saw where Robert Burns and his own true love lay side by side, covered by a simple marble monument. That was twenty years after that sister died; but when he stooped over the tomb where lay Burns and Jeanie side by side, the thought of the poet and of the sister came together, and the man wept like a child above that Scottish tomb. I only relate this anecdote as an illustration of the power that the memory and the appreciation of Burns holds in every civilized country of the world.

I said, sir, that I represent not Old Scotland, but New Scotland. All through that Province, and especially in the County of Pictou, which contains 20,000 Scotchmen, those who reverence his memory will do honor to it to-night. Your country and mine are divided into earnest and antagonistic parties; but such festivals as these are the soothing and humanizing spots of life, and the more of them the better. You have established between my country and yours commercial reciprocity. I hope to see the day when we shall have intellectual reciprocity—when I shall be able to invite the "Autocrat of the Breakfast Table" to Halifax; when Mayor Lincoln will come to Halifax and show us the light of his countenance; and also our friend Emerson, the philosopher of Concord,—and, upon my soul, all I can say of him is, he is the most agreeable and delightful philosopher I ever met. (Laughter.) I hope he will make his appearance in the British Provinces; and as to my friends Hillard and Lowell—let them all come, and we shall be delighted to receive them; they are known there already; they have flung their shadows far over the border. (Applause.)

Now, Mr. Chairman and Gentlemen, I fear I have trespassed upon you too long; but all I can say is, (as is sometimes done upon the gallows,) this is my last dying speech (laughter); the steamer sails to-morrow morning at twelve o'clock (renewed merriment); and when once I am out of New England you perhaps will never see me again, (shouts of "No! No!") I tell you what—occasionally the cholera comes; sometimes you have a bad harvest; sometimes you have a monetary pressure; and when you are thinking of your sins, and of all the bad things that may happen to you, just bear this in mind—it is possible that Howe may come back. (Hilarious laughter and cheering.)

8. *The Poet and the Press*—From the ingleside at Idlewild we observe the man who wields with equal power the wand of poesy and the pen of journalism.

The PRESIDENT. I have now the pleasure of introducing to you a gentleman of whom I may perhaps say, with justice, that he is the most popular literary man of New England—N. P. WILLIS, Esq. (Applause.) I am reminded that I have made a mistake, and I am called upon to say New York; but I do not stand corrected, for New England will never give up her right to him. (Loud applause.)

SPEECH OF N. P. WILLIS, ESQ.

MR. CHAIRMAN AND GENTLEMEN: For the last three or four days I have been unable to speak in an audible voice. Your good cheer, as you perceive, strengthens my feeble organs; but the gift of gab has been denied me from my earliest days. I have never been able to say, except at the point of my fingers, with a pen in my hand, what I wish to express. This is a vain effort for me. I am entirely unable to tell you what I should like to say. I can only thank you for the kind expression of your feelings toward me, and express my keen sense of the honor that is done me, and my appreciation of the beautiful heads and countenances that I see around me—the men whom I have appreciated, and of whom I have been in a certain degree the organ, the exponent, and by whom I am honored in having been their exponent. I warmly sympathize with the occasion, and appreciate the courtesy of the Boston Burns Club towards me.

[From one of the "Idlewild Letters," published in the *Home Journal*, we glean the following extracts, expressive of the thoughts he said he could better express with the pen than with the tongue :—]

In this century-honor to the Burns heart—in the recognition of the honest Burns humanity, by the entire world, as a hundred-year-memory which it would fain make immortal—there was something, it seemed to me, inexpressibly thrilling. I loved the world better for it, and I wanted to take part in it. Of such a "girdle round the earth" one wishes to help pass the electricity.

The main errand of my trip to Boston (the week's absence from home of which this letter is to give you some account) is thus explained to you. I wished to see them rock the memory of the Burns baby in my own cradle of first principles. I wished to be present at such a gathering of the "Boston boys"—to see their familiar faces and hear their remembered voices under that fine inspiration. With my pilgrim experience of life, and my farther knowledge of that world to which the dear old city was the encouraging vestibule, I wished to take to my heart, once more, the music of the God-speed. Where I first learned to read Burns and to love him, I wished to hear them talk of him again.

The most of what I heard and saw is, of course, already told to you. Of the "Burns Festival," as held in Boston, "the papers"—those brushers of the dew from all manner of herb and flower—have well given you the freshness. Taking it for granted, therefore, that you know all about it—that Tyler's speech and Waldo Emerson's, Hillard's and Joseph Howe's, Governor Banks' and Lord Radstock's, Lowell's poem, Whittier's and the Autocrat's, are all familiar to you—I shall look out of the corners of my own eyes for a moment or two, touching here and there a point where the light or shade chanced to fall better for my nearer seeing.

* * * * * * *

Speaking of Emerson, it was my good fortune to sit very near him at the dinner, and I could not but study the problem of his wonderful magnetism over his audience. Finely as his speech reads, in the newspaper report, (and never were more good things put into the same number of words,) the presentment of it in print, as compared with its effect in delivery, is poor. Why, in that large and convivially excited audience, there was not, while he spoke, a wandering eye—not a pulse or a breath that was not held absolutely captive. Wherein lies the wonderful spell? Between me and Emerson sat ten times as handsome a fellow—the young Englishman, Lord Radstock, with every pore and muscle in absolute health and development—yet, the excellent speech he, in his turn, delivered, was not a twentieth part as well attended to. Emerson has prodigiously strong will, for one thing—his lower jaw, as he grows older, betraying, by the hardening of the lines, what a lever of mental energy is there at work; and perhaps his voice, in partaking of this, has a natural emphasis of authority. But, in his whole personal presence, there is a charm—something more than the strong meaning of his words can well account for—a seignory of magnetism over other men's blood and nerve, the secret of which, it seems to me, might well be a study for the ambitious. How vague and unreal is any literary fame to such tangible sovereignty of presence!

Three of my immediate neighbors at the table were very bright spirits—George Hillard, Russell Lowell, and Autocrat Holmes—and, in the course of the five hours' symposium, there was a great deal of good talking, of course, that is not "down in the book." Of the exceedingly fine edge of Hillard's mind you would form some idea, perhaps, by reading the beautiful analysis of Burns' genius given in his speech; and you may see the quality of the other two men in the sparkling poems which are reported as they were read to us; but, for the enjoyment of all three by the audience, it was a pity that the recitations should not have given place to conversation. What a night we could have made of it, if these two hundred and fifty pairs of appreciative ears and responsive voices could all have been brought within chatting distance! What a limited science is acoustics, when no more than ten or fifteen persons can exchange the conversational accents which are alone the medium of wit!

I see by the papers that Mr. Spurgeon's congregation in London are about building him a church which shall be so acoustically constructed that he may have an audience much larger than has been hitherto thought possible. Why may not the improvements extend to dining-rooms? As we sat at our table in Boston, receiving, by electric telegraph, the toasts which were being drunk, at that moment, in distant cities, I felt prepared for almost any wonder of communication. We shall yet have Holmes sparkling off his wit for hundreds at a time—his conversation, which is the true bailiwick of his genius, extending gradually, perhaps, to the circulation of a newspaper! The "Atlantic," at present, is without the true "cable" for the Doctor.

The PRESIDENT. Gentlemen, we are honored with the presence here, this evening, at our table, of one of the peers of Ireland, and in our devotion to the thistle, we should not forget the shamrock. (Applause.) I have the pleasure of introducing to you Lord RADSTOCK.

SPEECH OF LORD RADSTOCK.

MR. PRESIDENT AND GENTLEMEN OF THE BURNS CLUB: It has given me great pleasure to take part in the festivities of this evening, not only because I was glad to have an opportunity to express my sense of the kindness with which I have been received in this country, but also because I believed there was at the bottom of this meeting to-night a deeper meaning, a deeper sentiment than has yet, I think, notwithstanding the oratory and poetry to which we have listened, been adequately expressed; and however imperfectly I may be able to express it, I shall try to suggest it to your minds, because I believe it to be important. That sentiment is, that a common literature produces union of sentiment, and strengthens the common objects of the two nations. If any proof was wanting up to this night that this was the case, it is wanting no longer.

I see that I am surrounded by gentlemen of the highest character and intellect, who honor English literature, and it is very gratifying to me to think that our common tastes and common sympathies are moulded upon the same model; and when we consider what the great destinies of the Anglo-Saxon race are, I am sure you will agree with me that the more we can stand shoulder to shoulder, and unite in feeling and action, the more will it result to the prosperity of ourselves and the advancement of mankind. (Applause.)

Gentlemen, what we have heard this night must teach us that we must endeavor to rely very much upon a common literature. It is that which strengthens the union, which teaches us to look for common interests and objects. Our common interests are certainly increase, advancement, progression; our common objects are not merely selfish or national, but world-wide. Great as is the influence of the Anglo-Saxon race now, we are numerically but a drop in the bucket—but fifty millions to the nine hundred millions on the globe; and the Anglo-Saxon race will not have performed its destiny until those nine hundred millions have felt something of the thrill which goes through the Anglo-Saxon heart. (Applause.)

It is on this account that I feel warranted in bringing forward this subject, important as I believe it to be, this night. And it was well expressed by the greatest man this country has ever produced, George Washington, who, when he laid down his military commission, said it was a free cultivation of literature, it was an unbounded extension of commerce, it was a progressive refinement of manners, it was a growing liberality of sentiment, and, above all, it was the light of a pure and benign revelation, which has had an ameliorating influence upon mankind.

If that was his verdict for the past, let it be our watchword for the future, and in our struggle for right against wrong, and truth against error, let us take that as our watchword, and then we shall be not only successful for ourselves, but be able to impart to the uncivilized portions of the world something of those blessings which we receive from a common literature and a common Christianity. (Loud applause.)

The next regular toast was then read:—

9. *Our dear old Home, the good City of Boston*—May prosperity ever attend her. (Cheers.)

The PRESIDENT then introduced, with appropriate remarks, His Honor FREDERIC W. LINCOLN, Jr., Mayor of the City, who spoke as follows:—

SPEECH OF MAYOR LINCOLN.

MR. PRESIDENT: I am sure, my dear sir, if there ever was an occasion where I had a right to be silent, it is at the present festival. It is not a civic feast which loads this table, or official functionaries who surround your board. The genius of poesy and literary culture embalm this atmosphere, and remarks from me seem ill-timed,—out of place.

My personal relation to the city which you have remembered in your sentiment, makes it my duty to respond. I shall do so briefly, and trespass but little on your patience.

I know of no particular associations connecting the memory of Burns and the city of Boston, excepting the fact that, distinguished as the city is for the love of literature, it embraces among its citizens some of the warmest admirers of the bard. The fact that we are assembled here to-night is significant of the respect that is paid to his memory, and of the estimation in which his writings are held. That his character as a man had many weak points we do not seek to conceal, but his instincts were noble, and the spirit of his poetry is to elevate and sweeten the joys of life.

Born and living all his days in the humblest circumstances, all ranks bow in homage to his genius, and he has left a name and exerted an influence which the titled and the great of the earth might envy.

At the age of sixteen he said love made him a poet, and that sentiment, more than any other, breathes in his muse, and draws him so closely to every heart. His poetry is so natural that we do not criticise it as a work of art; we are touched by its simplicity without knowing what moves us.

An anecdote is told of a lady who was one of his early patrons, who had a housekeeper who was surprised at the attention paid by her mistress to the rustic bard. The lady gave her a manuscript copy of the "Cottar's Saturday Night" to read, and asked her what she thought of it. She replied, "Very well." "Is that all you have to say in its favor?" asked the mistress. She said, "Yes, he had only described what had happened in her ain faither's house, and she didna ken how he could have described it ony ither gate."

The old woman thus paid him a compliment which more pleased the poet than if it had come from the most accomplished of literary critics.

The merit of his writings, and that which has made them so dear to people, is the absence of all the artificial distinctions of life, and the hearty recognition of the common brotherhood of man.

His noble thoughts have sustained many an humble laborer and peasant in their hours of toil, while they have afforded a rich intellectual enjoyment to the most cultivated minds.

But, sir, I will forbear. I remember what Burns, on his death-bed, said to a fellow-member of his military corps, "Don't let the awkward squad fire over me." I seem now to be disobeying his injunction, and will close by proposing as a sentiment—

The Natal Day of Burns—Ever to be remembered while the human heart vibrates to the touch of true poetry, or the bosom throbs with the noblest sympathy of our nature.

SONG—"Highland Mary."

The 10th regular toast was then given:—

Health to the sex, ilk guid chiel says,
Wi' merry dance in winter days,
Are we to share in common
The gust of joy, the balm of woe,
The soul of life, the heaven below,
Is rapture-giving woman.

The PRESIDENT called on Hon. JOSIAH QUINCY, Jr. to respond.

SPEECH OF HON. JOSIAH QUINCY, JR.

Our friend, Mr. Howe, told us that he was obliged to speak for all North America, and Scotland into the bargain. I have to speak for one half of creation, and that the better half. I shall not endeavor to say anything in this assembly in praise of the ladies. You have heard all the poetic and eloquent men who have preceded me speak concerning what we vulgarly call the lords of creation. Let them magnify them to the utmost; I will only ask you to remember the words of the bard:—

"Auld Nature swears, the lovely dears
Her noblest work surpasses, O;
Her prentice han' she tried on man,
And then she made the lasses, O."

But it is not, Mr. President, of the ladies in general that I would speak now, but, very briefly, of the particular female influences that made Burns a great poet. Among these, he speaks himself of one Jenny Wilson, who, he says, was superstitious and ignorant; who had no recommendation except the power of telling stories; that she was full of stories of ghosts, goblins, and witches. How much, sir, are we indebted to that Jane Wilson! I will not make a long quotation, but I think that about this time of night it would be well to give the moral of one of her stories:—

"Now wha this tale of truth shall read,
Ilk man and mither's son take heed;
Whene'er to drink you are inclined,
Or cutty sarks run in your mind,
Think ye may buy the joys o'er dear,
Remember Tam O'Shanter's mare."

But why are we assembled here to-night? We are assembled here because, as has already been said, a hundred years ago to-night, in a mud-walled cottage, which fell down a few days after, a woman rejoiced that a man-child was born into the world. And what was the influence of that woman? It has been very often inquired why it happens that so few great men leave great descendants after them. I believe that one reason is that talent is generally inherited from the mother. In my early youth it was my good fortune to live in the vicinity of that man to whom this country was perhaps more indebted for its constitution and liberty, than to any other in her history, excepting Washington. I refer to John Adams. I had the privilege of reading to him, and writing for him, quite frequently, and I remember very well that he asked me, on one occasion, what work I had been reading. I told him the life of Sir William Jones, and I spoke of the remarkable talent and power of the mother of that great man. "Young man," said he, "did you ever read or hear of a great and good man who had not a good mother? for I never did." And, sir, I believe we owe a great deal of the power of Burns to that mother. We are told that he resembled her physically, that she sung songs to him in his childhood, and many of his poems were written from tunes not now in existence, which he only remembered from having heard his mother sing them.

I will give a sentiment, which I have no doubt that, if the immortal poet could be cognizant of the meeting this evening, he would receive with more gratification than any sentiment that has been pronounced here to-night:—

The Mother of Robert Burns—The strains that she sung at his cradle are echoed through the world! (Loud applause.)

The PRESIDENT. It has already been stated that our Club is indebted to Miss Isabella Begg, a niece of the poet, for the contribution of various interesting articles. They were accompanied by the following letter:—

Letter from Miss Begg, a Niece of Robert Burns.

Bridgehouse, Ayr, 18th December, 1858.

Sir,—I regret your communication has been so long unnoticed, but it came just two days after my poor mother had breathed her last.

I will not damp your joy with our sorrow, for the wail that has been over the land for her, shows how deeply Burns has impressed the hearts of his fellow-men. I have seen many an unbidden tear fall from the eyes of strangers, when they looked upon his aged sister.

I am sorry I have so little to send you, but if the enclosed can be of any use, pray accept them. The card was written for a Bazaar a few years ago. I send also the signatures of the poet's three sons. Robert died in May, 1857. William Nicol and James Glencairn are both alive. James used always (on their annual visit here) to sing my dear mother one of his father's songs. For years, her request has n,

"Ca' the yowes to the knowes."

If any one at your great gathering will sing it in its beautiful native simplicity, you will thereby compliment the poet, his sister and his son. Accept also of a photograph taken a few weeks ago of my mother.

I wish I could have sent you the hand-writing of Burns, but this I cannot. With sincere wishes that you may have a happy meeting on the 25th of January, believe me,

Yours truly, ISABELLA BEGG.

Mr. John C. Moore, Secretary of the Boston Burns Club.

The following are the lines of Mrs. Begg, inscribed on a Card, mentioned in the above letter:—

"Life is but a day at most,
Sprung from night, in darkness lost,
Hope not sunshine every hour,
Fear not clouds will always lower."

The PRESIDENT then added this sentiment:—

We sympathize in feelings of natural affection, whilst we rejoice that the Poet is immortal.

Miss Begg's request in regard to the song of "Ca' the yowes to the knowes," was complied with by Mr. MOODY, who, a Scotchman, and an ardent admirer of Burns, rendered it in that simple, unaffected style in which it can only be properly sung. The song was loudly applauded.

The following letter was received from Hon. CALEB CUSHING:—

Letter from Gen. Cushing.

Boston, January 25, 1859.

My Dear Sir,—It is with extreme regret that I have to forego the pleasure of being with you this evening, as I had expected to be. I have hurt my eye so badly, that I have to put myself in the physician's hands. I wish you and your friends all possible enjoyment of this interesting occasion: and I am

Faithfully yours, C. CUSHING.

John S. Tyler, Esq.

Mr. Ordway's vocal band sang "Highland Mary" in capital style—Mr. Kelly being the soloist.

SPEECH OF WILLIAM CARRUTHERS, ESQ.

WILLIAM CARRUTHERS, Esq., of Salisbury, Mass., being introduced as a native of Dumfries, Scotland, spoke as follows:—

MR. PRESIDENT:—I had hoped to have heard some native of Scotland speak for her, but the task has been left to me. It was my lot in my early days to be familiar with everything connected with the closing scenes of the life of him whose birth we this night celebrate. At the time of his death, my father, then a young man, was one of those who made up the ten or twelve thousand who marched mournfully, step by step, with the chief mourners, as they bore away all that was mortal of the immortal Burns from the Trades' Hall to his last resting place in the old kirk yard of Dumfries. And in after years, when I was but a boy, it was my lot to follow that grand and imposing masonic procession which marched from the new kirk to the old, to lay the foundation stone of that mausoleum his admiring countrymen have erected to his memory. Knowing these facts, sir, you will not be surprised to find me here to-night, and that I am not an uninterested spectator of all that has passed before me. Mr. President, I have listened with inexpressible delight to those gentlemen who stand stand so high in the literary world, as they have this night spoken "in prose and rhyme" of Burns and of my native country. From the bottom of my heart I thank them. I am convinced, sir, that we, as Scotchmen even, have not yet begun, much as we love the Rustic Bard, to appreciate him. We have loved him, and do love him, for his songs, for they speak the language of the heart; but we have not as yet esteemed him as the one that has best given expression to those feelings of liberty and freedom that have burned in the bosom of every true son of Scotia since the days of Wallace and Bruce. (Cheers.) Permit me to state an incident that occurred in Dumfries, about the year 1792. Burns being in a large, mixed company, the health of William Pitt was proposed. He gave great offence by demurring, and left the room in indignation because they would not substitute another name. And what name was that, sir? Let me give you his toast in his own words: "The health of a greater and a better man, *George Washington!*" And be it known, sir, that this was said and done when Burns was an exciseman, or, in other words, a custom-house officer, under that same William Pitt, prime minister of England. (Loud cheers.)

We Scotchmen love Burns not less for his songs, but more for that love of liberty and the rights of man which stand out in such bold relief through all his works, and nowhere better expressed than in these memorable lines:—

> "The rank is but the guinea's stamp,
> The man's the gowd for a' that." (Cheers.)

And permit me, sir, in closing, to say, that though this land of my adoption has been my home for upwards of forty years, and is the home and the birthplace of my children, yet I cannot help it, (and if I could I would not,) there is still in this heart of mine a warm side to the heathery hills and broomy knowes of my native land. (Loud cheers.)

Mr. President, one word to my countrymen, and then I have done. Let us, in this land of our adoption, act worthy of the home of our childhood; let the influence of the Hearth, the School and the Kirk, be felt wherever we go, for it is

> "From scenes like these old Scotia's grandeur springs,
> That make her loved at home, revered abroad;"

and let the green holly of Scotland rustle with the majestic pine of the Old Bay State, in united effort to do all we can to bring about that glorious time, for which he, whose memory we this night celebrate, so fervently prayed—

> "When freedom's treasures shall be free as air,
> And slave and despot be but things that were."

Mr. Carruthers took his seat amid the warm applause of the company.

OTIS RICH, Esq., Vice-President of the Club, after a few well-conceived introductory remarks, gave the following sentiment, which was properly honored :—

The Genius of Robert Burns—It has not only cheered the hearthstones of the lowly cottages of his native land, but has inspired the good and great of all countries, wherever true poetry is appreciated, to unite this day in such a demonstration to his memory and his fame, as was never paid to literary talent in any age of the world. May we long feel the hallowing influence of his poetry, and may his name be ever cherished.

The regular toasts and sentiments having been exhausted at this point, volunteers were numerous, heartfelt and appropriate. Songs and brief speeches followed in rapid succession—including expressions of gratitude to the President and officers of the Club for the liberal manner in which they had brought the proceedings of the festival to a completion. Nor were Messrs. Parker & Mills forgotten in the list of compliments paid.

"The wee short hour ayont the twal" had closely invaded the precincts of its successor ere the idea of rising became anything like general. A few minutes before two o'clock the President rose and suggested that "Auld Lang Syne" should be sung, and that afterwards the festival should close. This was complied with, and "the banquet hall deserted" immediately thereafter.

The following letters and messages were read during the evening. To the telegraphic despatches prompt replies were given through the same media by which they came. In this connection it is proper to say that the Club were placed under obligations to the northern lines of telegraph through their voluntary offer to send despatches free—a privilege which was made available to a very liberal extent :—

LETTER FROM HUGH MUIR.

Wrightfield, Alloway, Ayrshire, Scotland, Dec. 16, 1858.

MR. JOHN C. MOORE, BOSTON:

Dear Sir,—I cannot describe with what pleasure I sit down to write you a few lines. Much I could say, but this is not the time. I have sent you two small relics, which are of very little value, but I can vouch that they are what the tickets represent them to be. With regard to the little piece of wood, you will recollect a fine plane tree, planted inside the sacred old walls of Kirk Alloway, which grew near

"The winnock bunker in the East,
Where sat Auld Nick in shape o' beast."

The roots got underneath the walls, and in a short time would have thrown them, or part of them, down. I have had the charge of the place for a number of years, and pointed out to the managers, at one of their meetings, the danger to the walls, and I was ordered to cut the tree down. You may make what use of the piece of it I send that you please.

The small piece of iron I send you is of more value. I took it out of the south door of the Auld Kirk, which has lately been removed, and an iron gate put in its place.

Yours truly, HUGH MUIR.

LETTER FROM DAVID CAMPBELL.

High Street, Ayr, Dec. 21, 1858.

Dear Sir,—Having heard, through my friend Mr. Grant, of your wish to collect some relics of Burns for your Centennial meeting, I have much pleasure in sending you a photograph of the late Mrs. Begg, taken by me at her residence a few weeks before her death, and also a stereograph of the Cottage, Alloway Kirk, the Monument, and the old Bridge of Doon, and I shall feel obliged by your kindness in presenting them to the members of the Boston Burns Club, with my compliments.

I am, &c., DAVID CAMPBELL.

MR. JOHN C. MOORE, Sec'y of the Boston Burns Club.

LETTER FROM THEO. CHAMBERLIN.

Cincinnati, Jan. 19, 1859.

COL. WM. SCHOULER, BOSTON:

It is made my very pleasant duty to return, through you, to the Burns Club of Boston, the warmest thanks of the Burns Club of Cincinnati, for their present of the copy of King's bust of the immortal Bard of Scotia. Assure your Club, in language you know so well how to use, and which pen cannot portray, of our grateful appreciation of their kindness in making the gift in so handsome a manner. And assure them, also, that we shall cherish the memento as a bond of lasting friendship between Boston and the Queen City, and that, in looking upon it, we shall have a better and warmer appreciation of Burns and his songs, of him as a man, and of his muse, world-charming and immortal, because our sister, Boston, has furnished us with the means of doing so.

Accept the best wishes of our Club for yours, and yourself, and believe me to be,

Very truly, your friend, THEODORE CHAMBERLIN,
Sec'y Cincinnati Burns Club.

MESSAGES BY TELEGRAPH.

Washington, Jan. 25, 1859.

TO JOHN C. MOORE:

The Washington Burns Club, at a full table, pledges the Boston Burns Club, and all others who honor this anniversary.

Per order, BEN. PERLEY POORE, *Sec'y.*

Revere House, Boston, Jan. 25.

TO THE PRESIDENT OF THE BOSTON BURNS CLUB:

Dear Sir,—I have the honor of informing you that the following toast, with all the honors, has just been drank by the party now at the Revere House, similarly engaged as yourselves, celebrating the birthday of Scotland's immortal bard:—

The Boston Burns Club—Success attend its efforts to perpetuate the memory of Robert Burns.

I am, dear sir, yours respectfully,
W. J. MCPHERSON, *Sec'y.*

Montreal, Jan. 25, 1859.

TO THE BURNS CLUB OF BOSTON:

The admirers of Burns, assembled in Montreal, send greetings to their Boston friends, and give:—

The Day, and a' wha honor it—Long may the memory of Burns live in the hearts of his countrymen and admirers.

A. A. STEVENSON, *Sec'y.*

New York, Jan. 25, 1859.

THE NEW YORK BURNS ASSOCIATION SENDS GREETING:

Peace to the ashes of the noble dead!
  The years of strife for glory haply o'er,
A century's halo now enwreaths his head,
  Who sang of love as minstrel ne'er before;
For still that harp with Scotland's glory wed
Thrills every heart where love its light hath shed:

Auld Scotia's sons, whatever clime they see,
Can never to his memory faithless be;
With them his fame shall go from shore to shore,
His name shall live till time shall be no more.
Love's purest offering shall surround his grave—
Love's sweetest incense ever round it wave.

JAMES GRAY, *Vice-President.*

Detroit, Mich., Jan. 25, 1859.

TO THE BOSTON BURNS CLUB:

The admirers of Robert Burns, now in social session, send to their brethren of the Boston Burns Club, greeting; and respectfully offer the following sentiment:—

Burns—The genial and patriotic poet of Scotland, who, by his devotion to his country and countrymen, best illustrated man's power to serve humanity.

ADAM ELDER, *President.*

New York, Jan. 25, 1859.

THE AULD LANG SYNE ASSOCIATION OF NEW YORK GREET THEIR BRETHREN OF THE BOSTON BURNS CLUB, AND GIVE—

The Old Folks at Home around the cheerful Firesides of Auld Scotland—There Scotia's bairns receive the first principles of honest, upright conduct, while with the ingleside is entwined the memories of the happy youthful days when we read the poems and sung the songs of our own Robert Burns!

WILLIAM HODGE.

Lowell, Jan. 25, 1859.

THE LOWELL BURNS CLUB TO THE BOSTON BURNS CLUB, GREETING:

The Lowell Burns Club send their heartiest greetings to their brethren in Boston, now socially assembled to do honor to the memory of "the world's poet," and offer as a sentiment the words of the lamented Tannahill, a brother poet:—

Robert Burns, the Patriot Poet.

"Yes, Burns, 'thou dear departed shade!'
When rolling centuries have fled,
Thy name shall still survive the wreck of time,
Shall rouse the genius of thy native clime;
Bards yet unborn, and patriots shall come
And catch fresh ardor at thy hallow'd tomb!"

PETER LAWSON, *President, Lowell Burns Club.*

Baltimore, Jan. 25, 1859.

TO THE BOSTON CLUB:

The Baltimore Burns Club to the Boston Burns Club, send best wishes, and give:—

The Day we Celebrate—The Hundredth Birthday of Robert Burns: a thousand years may pass, and still his name will live while earth for man has smiles and tears.

JAMES CAIRNS, *Secretary*.

Cincinnati, Jan. 25, 1859.

Boston and Liberty—True and living interpretations of American sentiment; may the former become foremost in the annals of prosperous cities, and the latter finally take captive the hearts of all civilized men!

THEO. CHAMBERLIN,
Secretary, Cincinnati Burns Club.

Quebec, Jan. 25, 1859.

The Committee of Management of the Burns Centenary Festival at Quebec, wish the Boston Burns Club to join their association in honoring the following sentiment:—

Burns—Scotia, with exulting tear, honors her son, and his admirers in Britain and America unite in paying deep and sincere homage to him, the bard that's awa.

J. DUNBAR, *Secretary*.

Manchester, N. H., Jan. 25, 1859.

THE MANCHESTER LITERARY SOCIETY TO THE BOSTON BURNS CLUB, GREETING:

The Scottish Bard—He lives in song; his love of liberty burns in the hearts of the people. Without regard to wealth, nation, or rank, may we endeavor

"That man to man the warld o'er
Shall brithers be an' a' that."

JOHN R. HYNES,
For Committee of Arrangements.

From the Burns Club of the City of Elms.

New Haven, Jan. 25, 1859.

TO THE BURNS CLUB AT THE PARKER HOUSE, BOSTON:

The City of Classic Shades greets the Literary Capital of the Union, which has brought the tribute of American genius to the memory of our national bard. May Boston ever stand preëminent for freedom, truth, and letters. May her sons of genius long live to elevate man and address the world, and in future times have their shrines, too, consecrated by the genius of other lands.

New York, Jan. 25, 1859.

TO THE BURNS CLUB OF BOSTON:

The Burns Clubs of Scotland, trickling in sweet music down the hill of time, gathering force, bear universal man towards realms of union, friendship, truth, and love.

J. L. DICK, *Chairman*.

From the New York Burns Anniversary Association.

New York, Jan. 25, 1859.

TO THE BOSTON BURNS CLUB:

Kindred Associations throughout the World—May they preserve the songs, and disseminate the sentiments, of Burns, till

"—— man to man the warld o'er
Shall brithers be an' a' that."

VAIR CLIREHUGH, JR., *Cor. Sec'y.*

Troy, N. Y., Jan. 25, 1859.

THE BURNS CLUB OF TROY, N. Y., TO THE BOSTON BURNS CLUB, GREETING:

Robert Burns—The bard whose immortal pen annihilated the principle that birth and rank were the conditions of honor, and promulgated for them that of worth.

Galveston, Texas, Jan. 25, 1859.

TO THE BOSTON BURNS CLUB, IN SOCIAL ASSEMBLY:

The Mountains of Scotland—Hallowed by the remembrance of the Scottish Chiefs.

The Hills and Valleys of New England—Sacred to the memory of the Pilgrim fathers; and

The Prairies of Texas—Once the hunting-ground of a despot, now the garden spot of the South, and gained by the aid of Cameron, a Scotchman.

A. J. RUTHVEN, *Chairman Burns Club.*

OFFICERS OF THE CLUB FOR 1859–60.

At the annual meeting of the Boston Burns Club, held in the Parker House, on Wednesday evening, February 2d, 1859, the following gentlemen were chosen officers of the Club for the year ensuing:—

President, . . . JOHN S. TYLER.
Vice President, OTIS RICH.
Treasurer, . . . WILLIAM BOGLE.
Librarian, . . . JUSTIN JONES.
Secretary, . . . JOHN C. MOORE.

CPSIA information can be obtained
at www.ICGtesting.com
Printed in the USA
LVHW100908250223
740367LV00002B/231

9 783382 308254